JB CAINE

STRENGTH
OF
WILL

Arcana Book 3

Dedication

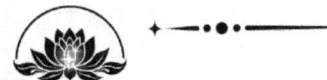

For Barbara.
Without you, the Arcana wouldn't be nearly so magical.
Thank you, thank you, thank you.

More by JB Caine

In the Arcana Trilogy:
Rise of the Moon
Rush to Judgement
Strength of Will
The Ironshield's Shadow Series
The Manifest Destiny Series (with Betsey Kulakowski)
The YOUR STORY Series

*E*nergy *harnessed and blood to blood.*

The Great Mage raised his arms.

Da formam virtutis. Give form to the Power.

A glow erupted from the chalk that outlined the circle and energy spiraled, sending the scent of rosemary into the swirling winds. All 22 voices gasped as their feet lifted from the ground and their sigils burned crimson on their arms.

The mounded circle of chalk was lifted into the swirling vortex and diverged into multiple smaller bands of light, undulating like the crown of Medusa.

Slowly, the beams of misty light lowered to the ground in a new configuration, a complex criss-cross, and each of the mages touched down simultaneously on separate lines. Light exploded skyward, and then complete darkness fell like gravity, extinguishing the fire and candles.

A moment of silence, and then the Great Mage's voice rang out through the inky night.

The deed is done, Brothers and Sisters. The Arcana is sealed in blood and fire.

Chapter 1

Normally, I fancy a solo road trip, but Aria's outburst at breakfast had me in a twist.

"What you are doing is WRONG," she had insisted. But it wasn't her words that shook me. It was the *glow.*

She had asked me about the new kid. Asked if I had inquired if he *wanted* to come to Atlanta. But then she held up her hands and her chakras lit up like a stack of Roman candles.

Chakras are central to my power as Strength, like seven little light bulbs of different colors running down the center of your body. Whenever Aria used her abilities as Judgment, her *ajna,* or third-eye chakra, would light up. Most of the time, it flickered in and out like a violet candle flame. As she sat staring at me over a bowl of yogurt and fruit, it was glowing and pulsating.

If her deity got involved, her crown chakra would light up, too. So far, I hadn't seen that happen, and with the stink eye I was getting right now, I was certain that was a good thing.

"What is so important that you're just cool with ripping people away from their families?" she asked me. She was getting angry, and that was to be expected since she was probably still homesick and hadn't fully settled in yet. But then the rest of her chakras started glowing and she held out her hands, palms up. Her *manipura*, her solar plexus chakra, grew brighter and brighter, and the energy began to leak out and create an aura of power over her hands. The golden glow was nearly blinding. Then that crown chakra started up, sending rays of violet light out like a disco ball. I tensed, expecting a blast of energy, my body preparing to dive in whatever direction looked safest. This was not a power she'd shown in training. How had the clever little brat hid this from me?

"What the hell are you doing with your hands?"

Her crown chakra began to intensify, and glow a bright purple. I wasn't sure what all of Judgement's powers were, but she was definitely calling to her deity. "It's not right, what you're doing," she told me. "You choose to be here, and that's cool, but you can't just go around collecting people who *don't* want to be here. That's *wrong*." The purple from the crown chakra at the top of her head began to spread into an aura enveloping her whole body.

Not her body. Another body. Her Goddess.

And then I felt something stripped away from me, like a veil over my eyes had been pulled back. My head filled with thoughts, feelings, doubts ... they were mine, and I recognized them, but suddenly I was *feeling them*. It was like characters had stepped out of a movie screen and were suddenly standing in front of me.

"What you are doing is WRONG."

My mind raced. Was she right? I mean, Dad was her father, too ... her mother was dead ... shouldn't she be with her father? Why wouldn't she want to grow up with a biological parent? And definitely this other kid, David, he'd rather be with Dad than the crap life he'd been living, right?

"Look, he's basically homeless, alright? He doesn't have anyone to miss him or anywhere to go. He's been bouncing around in the foster care system up there. We finally tracked him down. We're going to give him a *home*." It was all true … David was one of Dad's other Arcana kids; in fact, he was the youngest of us. Only 13, and he'd been in foster care for nearly two years. Four homes in that time. I'd been talking to him via text for nearly a month, and he was definitely on board with coming to Atlanta. What we were doing was a *good* thing!

"I already had a home." Aria's eyes sizzled at me. She was right. We'd basically kidnapped her. Threatened harm to the cousins and aunt who'd raised her if she didn't come willingly. *Oh my God, we kidnapped her.* But he was her dad … who wouldn't want to be with her own father? *What was happening to me?*

"Yeah, well, I don't know what to say about that," was all I was able to come up with. "I have to go." I grabbed my bag and headed for the door, but the voice in my head wouldn't keep mum. *What you are doing is WRONG.*

She was right. We'd caused a minor car crash to show her we were capable of hurting her family if she didn't come. *Why had I gone along with hurting someone?* And there was more. We had another sister, Lia, in Florida. And we'd nicked her, too, but her friend had rescued her. We'd been trying to figure out how to bring her back.

I was a kidnapper. Or at least an accessory. *What had I become? Why would I do this to other kids … my own brothers and sisters?* I turned back to look at Aria, and my heart hurt. I had to think, had to process all of this. "I'm sorry," I told her, then fled to my car.

I wasn't in a hurry. My plan was to hit I-85 and head northeast to Richmond, then pick up I-95 and take it all the way to New York. I already had a hotel reservation for two nights in Richmond. Unless traffic got in my way, I'd make it to the hotel early in the evening, maybe half-six, then I would have a good meal, watch a movie on my laptop, and take a good rest. Then I could cover the remaining distance and brave New York traffic the next day, snag the kid, and make it back to Richmond before it got too late.

The longer I drove, the better I started to feel. Dad had gone up and met my brother-to-be privately to introduce himself, then gave him a burner phone and told him to keep it stashed. I started texting him a few days later. David was only too happy to ditch the group home he was living in, he said, and we'd made arrangements for me to pick him up and bring him back to Atlanta.

See? No kidnapping. The kid was 100% on-board. *But what would have happened if he resisted? What would we have done then?*

I cursed myself for thinking too much, turned up the stereo, and started singing along to the banger on the satellite station. Just the thing to improve my sour mood. Like I said, I liked solo road trips. They felt like adventures and hey, if I was helping Dad out, so much the better.

The plan was to meet the kid outside the Staten Island Zoo on Wednesday afternoon around 2:00. His group home was in Brooklyn, but he assured me he'd have no problem cutting school and getting himself over to Staten Island. I didn't ask him how, but I got the impression he was a resourceful little nipper.

Sure enough, as I rolled down Broadway (not THE Broadway ... the one in Staten Island), I spotted him in his navy blue hoodie, carrying a backpack and watching the traffic pass by. He was standing along a chain-link fence in front of a brick house that looked like it would be beautiful if someone actually took care of the garden.

I took a moment to look him over. He was average in height, and lanky in that way only new teenagers can be: all knees and elbows. His dishwater-brown hair was a bit of a mop, and I wasn't sure if it was a style choice or that the foster system didn't spring for regular haircuts. His thumbs were tucked into the straps of a backpack which, apparently, served as both luggage and a cushion between the kid and the chain link fence. I navigated into a parallel spot and rolled down the window.

"Oy! David!"

He looked up with his pale eyes and started walking toward my car. Then he peered into the window. "You're Zora?" He sounded surprised.

"You expecting the mayor?"

"Nah, you just ain't what I thought."

"Wrong flavor?" Dad probably hadn't told him his big sister was Black. Typical.

He shrugged. "It's all good. Guess Dad got around."

"You could say that. You still coming with me?" I popped the lock open as an invitation.

"Hell, yeah, I am." He opened the door, slid in, and wedged his backpack between his feet. "So you have the same accent *he* does. You're British, too?"

"English, yeah. From London. Buckle up."

He rolled his eyes and his voice oozed sarcasm. "Yes, ma'am."

"Don't be so cringe. I need to deliver you in one piece."

"Or you don't get paid?"

"Paid? No. I'm your sister, not your chauffeur."

He grinned, and despite my general annoyance, the smile was infectious and I smiled back. "I guess you're alright," he announced. "Long as you're not too uptight, we'll get along."

"Gee, thanks." I threw the amused sarcasm right back at him. "I'll sleep so much better tonight."

That brought a laugh out of him. "Cool. Hey, there's a McDonald's up on the left. I'm in need of a Big Mac. Stat."

"Yeah, alright. I could do with a bite myself. But we aren't stopping for long. Just stopping for take-away and a wee, got it?"

"A what?"

I faked my best American accent, which was outright awful. "Take-out and the restroom."

"Oh. Why didn't you just say that?"

It was my turn to roll my eyes out loud.

Thirty minutes later, we were crossing the Goethals Bridge and heading for the New Jersey Turnpike in order to head back south to Richmond. David was still munching on his second order of large fries as we drove.

"So, like, this Dorian guy raised you?"

"Not so much when I was younger. I mean, he came round a good bit, and I've known him my whole life, but I didn't start living with him until I was about your age. When my mum got sick."

"So she died?" I was a little jarred by his directness.

"Yeah. Cancer."

"That sucks. My mom is dead, too. But she OD'd, though. Almost three years ago."

"It must've been very rough on you. I'm sorry."

He shrugged, his signature move, and it was apparent to me this one hid real pain behind nonchalance. "She was alright most of the time before she died. She didn't do a lot of drugs. But her back was hurting a lot, so she bought a painkiller from somebody in the neighborhood. The cops said it was laced with Fentanyl." He said it like he was giving me a news report.

"That's awful, that you lost her so suddenly." It wasn't hard to be sympathetic.

There was a long pause, then David spoke up again. "So which Card've you got?"

"Strength. And Dad is the Magician."

"Yeah, he told me. I'm the Devil."

"I'll just bet you are," I quipped as the miles rolled under our wheels.

Chapter 2

David hadn't been quiet for more than five minutes before his face lit up in a huge puckish grin. "What are your powers?"

"You ask a lot of questions, kid."

"It's a long drive."

"Fair. I have a few abilities I've been using for years. I can see chakras—which, before you ask, are energy centers in the body's electrical field—so I can see if someone's hiding something, I can tell if another Arcana is using their power, that sort of thing."

"That doesn't seem very useful. No offense."

"None taken, but you'd be surprised. It's very difficult to lie to me or take me by surprise, and that's actually quite useful." I wondered how much I should tell him. "And sometimes I can make myself physically stronger."

"Okay, now *that's* useful," he said appreciatively. I decided not to tell him I could sometimes compel people to do what I wanted them to. My mother hadn't been able to do that, but it was sort of Dad's specialty, so I figured I must have inherited some abilities from him.

Suddenly, my argument with Aria flashed across my mind. Dad was an expert at mind control. *Is that why I've gone along with kidnapping people?*

Whatever Aria had done to me had awakened a Jiminy Cricket voice in my brain, and it wasn't about to be silenced. I didn't have time for it at that moment, however.

"What about you?" I asked. "What powers does the Devil have?"

"A ridiculous amount of charm," he chuckled. "Hey, don't hit that thing in the road."

I looked where he had pointed, but saw nothing. "Are you trying to use suggestion on me? Because it definitely didn't ..." I gasped when I glanced over at him. Instead of the sandy-haired, blue-eyed boy who'd been sitting next to me a moment ago, I was looking at a boy with black hair and eyes, with the rich brown skin I was used to seeing in people from the southern part of India. The clothes were the same, but the face bore no resemblance to the one I'd been looking at for the last hour. His solar plexus chakra was glowing like polished brass.

"Gotcha," he snickered. And with a shake of his head, the familiar face returned. "I can glamour pretty good. That's what Mom called it. And I really do have a boatload of charm when I want to. I can talk people into stuff. How do you think I got to Staten Island?"

"Those are very useful skills. Who is your deity?"

"He calls himself Coyote."

"Coyote? Like the animal?"

"Well, sort of. He says lots of native cultures recognize Him. He's pretty cool. Sometimes He answers me and sometimes not. He likes to go exploring. But when He does talk to me, He gives me some fun ideas."

"Like what kinds of ideas?" Devilish ideas could be a dangerous thing. I wanted to know what quagmire we were getting ourselves into with young David.

"Pranks, mostly. And how to skip out on stuff, or how to get something I want. I don't know. But sometimes He takes a liking to someone and has me help them. He's kind of hard to predict."

"That doesn't sound very Devilish."

David sat up very tall, or at least as tall as a skinny 13-year-old was able, and I could tell he was about to give me his version of an education.

"The Devil card doesn't always mean evil. I mean, it might for some people, but what it really means is *chaos*. The Devil doesn't like rules. That's how the Christian Devil was made. He was an Archangel who wouldn't follow the rules. Devils do things our own way. Sometimes people see that as evil, but it doesn't have to be."

"I have the suspicion you've heard that same speech before."

"Yeah, when Mom died, I didn't know much about the Card. I mean I knew she could talk people into almost anything. And she never took crap from anybody. She had shown it to me when I was little, and told me it was magic. But I reckon she wasn't planning on dying so young, so she didn't explain much to me."

"How did you learn about it?"

"Coyote explained some of it to me. He said there's other stuff I can do, too, and He'll teach me about it when He thinks I'm ready. He says I can make fire, but I'm still too much of a kid to learn that part. I think that's BS. He should teach me. I'm not a stupid kid." As he talked about the fire, I perceived his throat chakra flickering slightly.

"You're lying," I said flatly. "Or at least not telling the whole truth."

He gave me his most charming smile, and I felt like I'd won a prize somehow. "Very cool," he complimented me. "You're right. I taught myself to make fire because He wouldn't." More flickering.

"Still lying. Try again."

"Nice. Okay, no cap, I've been trying to learn how to make fire, but I haven't been able to. Not yet." No flickering.

"Thank you. Now was that so hard?"

"Oh, no, not hard at all. How else am I supposed to learn how to trick your Spidey Sense?"

I gave him a hard side-eye, and he winked and popped a tepid fry in his mouth.

We had a nice dinner in Richmond, then returned to the hotel room. We watched a horror movie, and afterwards, David dug into his backpack and pulled out the change of clothes he'd brought with him: a black tee shirt with a wolf outlined in blue, a pair of socks, and a pair of boxers

"I'm gonna need clothes. This was all I could bring. I didn't have a lot more anyway, but I …"

"What do you say we hit a store on the way back to Atlanta? We can pick up a few things for you."

There was a spark of something in his eyes as he looked at me. Like maybe he'd expected to have to talk me into it, like maybe people didn't just offer him nice things without a dose of persuasion. Then he shrugged. "That'd be cool. Thanks."

The traffic in the Raleigh-Durham area of North Carolina was beastly on the way through, so I figured that was as good a place as any for our shopping trip. I pulled into the parking lot of a big-box store. I saw a light in David's eyes which reminded me of Christmas, but I couldn't really tell if it was gratitude or greed. Maybe a little of both. It didn't sound like he'd had an easy life, so I kind of wanted to show him what was possible.

Maybe he'd be happy with us and there'd be one fewer sibling to kidnap. *Did I truly just normalize kidnapping my brothers and sisters? What is WRONG with me?*

"Okay, listen, I'm not Moneybags McGee here. You can pick six clothing items. Your choice, but six is the limit. Anything else will have to come from Dad, okay?" I mean, technically this was coming from Dad, too, since it was his credit card I'd be using, but being the oldest sibling meant being at least moderately responsible.

"Any six things I want?"

"Any six *clothing items* you want. You can even make one of them a pair of shoes. But I'm not bankrolling toys or any of that rubbish, got it?"

He looked at me for a minute with his trademark smirk, and I was just sure he was going to try and bargain. Then he seemed to think the better of it. "Okay, six. Got it."

For a while, I followed him through the boys' clothing section, and despite its fairly limited size, he seemed to be taking an unnecessary amount of time choosing. "Are you looking for something specific?" I asked him, hoping to gently hurry him along.

"I mean, I dunno. I like what I like. You don't have to babysit me. Why don't you go look at make-up or something?"

"Do I look like I give a rip about make-up? Seriously? What patriarchal rock are you living under?" I couldn't remember the last time I'd worn makeup. My vanity stopped at the tips of my locs.

"I just mean you can go look at stuff you want. It makes me feel weird with you following me around anyway. I don't exactly want to shop for tighty-whities with someone I just met."

"Fair enough," I acceded. "I'm going to go look at the magazines and go to the bathroom, which you should also do before we hit the road again, by the way. You have 30 minutes to pick your six and meet me at the registers."

"Cool." A strange rainbow effect, like light shining through a many-faceted crystal, swept across his aura. I raised an eyebrow, not sure what to make of it. Is that what auras look like when people are happy?

"Cool," I said back, then made my way over to the magazines to see if I could find any new anime comics. I browsed for several minutes, but didn't find anything that set me alight, so I started heading for the front of the store to use the loo and wait for David.

I didn't make it very far before a hefty fellow in a uniform labeled SECURITY stopped me.

"'Scuse me, miss. Are you Zora Blair?"

Oh, bloody hell. What did that kid do? "I am. How can I help you, officer?"

"There's a young man in our office claiming you're his sister. Is that accurate?" He looked at me skeptically. I couldn't blame him. We didn't have much family resemblance.

"Half-sister, but yeah. Is David okay?"

"Can you come with me, please?" This store cop — Ray, according to his name badge — was being way too calm and way too polite. David definitely wasn't hurt, but he was most decidedly in trouble. My bet was on shoplifting.

My bet was right. I should play the ponies.

When the guy led me into the security office, David was sitting at a table, his beloved backpack wide open and WAY more than six items spread out on the table. His eyes were downcast, and when he saw me walk in he broke into heart-wrenching sobs. The other security officer looked more sheepish than angry, which wasn't what I expected.

"David, what's what here?" I tried to sound brusque without losing my temper.

He snuffled and looked up, and real tears were streaming down his face. "I—I know you said I could pick six things—I'm sorry, I just—" He buried his face in his hands, and the security guard who had been waiting with him pulled out a bandana and handed it to the kid. He looked up at the guy and accepted it, mopping his face and wiping his nose. "Thank you. Zora, I'm sorry. I—I've never gotten to go shopping before, and it was wrong, but—" *sniffle, sniffle,* "I just—I've always had to look out for myself, you know? No one ever gave me nothin'. Please don't make me go back!" He buried his sobs in his handkerchief, and Ray looked very uncomfortable.

I was uncomfortable too, but not because of David's waterworks. It was because I had to talk our way out of this without creating a paper trail.

Because technically, at least as far as the law would see it, I had kidnapped David.

DAMN IT. There it is again! How does this keep happening to me?

Dad had located him and talked to him privately. We had given him a phone, and he had agreed to come live with us. We hadn't done one lick of legal paperwork. Not one. It had seemed like no big deal at the time. David was our blood, and he wanted to live with us. If we *had* gone through legal channels, the result would have been the same, but David would have probably been stuck in the foster system for at least another year. Why put him through that?

But now I was on the hook, and had to make this work somehow.

"I'm sorry, officers. this is going to be hard to believe, but—" I reached into my own power and activated my throat chakra. I pushed blue light outward until it filled the room, willing the security guards to *feel* my words. "David is my brother. Our father and his mother, well, you know … and we only recently learned about him and were able to track him down. His mother died, you see, and the poor kid has been in foster care. We were so happy we found him, so we could bring him home to be with us." David started audibly bawling into the bandana. "And, I know what he did was wrong; he knows it, too. We're trying so hard to give him a second chance. Do you have any idea what group homes are like?" Not-Ray the security guard was getting choked up, and I knew my magic was working. "Look, I'll pay for everything he nicked. Please. I don't want to land you lot in trouble or anything, but is there anything we can do to keep him from getting arrested?"

"What do you think, Ray?"

I turned to look at Ray, and he looked shaken. My juju had whallopped him. "Listen, little dude," he said to David, "I was a foster kid, too." Bleary-eyed, David looked up from the hanky, his eyes shining with hope. "Don't mess this up. If you have a good family to claim you, you gotta get right, son. Most of us never got that chance."

David nodded mutely, then looked at me like I was some kind of angel. He wouldn't be thinking that in about ten minutes, that was for sure.

"Alright, miss, look. You pay for the items he picked up, and we'll call it square. No harm, no foul. But listen, kid — David, is it? — You keep your nose clean, okay?"

David nodded enthusiastically, but wisely kept his trap shut.

Three shirts, one pair of jeans, a gaming magazine, four packs of peanut butter cups, and five packs of Pokémon cards later, we were bagged up and walking out of the store under the watchful eyes of Ray and not-Ray.

Once we were safely sitting back in the car, I turned to him, my eyes and temper on fire.

"Now listen, you git—"

"That. Was. AWESOME!" He was grinning ear to ear. "You had them eating outta your freaking HAND!"

"That was most definitely NOT awesome! You took a huge gamble, and I paid the damn price! What the bloody hell got into you?"

He laughed out loud, all traces of his glamour-tears completely gone from his cheeks. "Are you kidding me? You were so *clutch*! You—"

"I told them the truth is what I did! You were the one putting on the show. What if I'd decided to deny even knowing you?"

He chuckled again. "Ah, I'd have been alright. North Carolina can't be any tougher than New York. You knew I was faking that whole time?"

"Of course I did. I told you."

"You have really good Spidey Sense. I didn't even lie, so I didn't think you'd know it was an act."

"You didn't have to lie. You were still being deceptive. Don't underestimate my power, David. And now I don't trust you anymore, so you can bet I'll be on guard. Once we get home, you're Dad's problem. And if you think I'm powerful, you have no idea what he's like. Don't try to pull this kind of crap with him."

"Yeah, yeah, okay." He still seemed totally chuffed with himself. My heart filled with dread. This wouldn't go over well with Dad. I hoped the kid wouldn't try any tricks at home, but I had a feeling there was a lot of trouble brewing. "How'd you figure it out, anyway?"

"Like I'd tell you any more about how my powers work. Forget it." I certainly wouldn't tell him his crown chakra, the one that connected him to his deity, had been glowing so brightly it almost hurt me to look at it.

I had a pretty strong sense that Coyote and Dad weren't going to get along at all.

Chapter 3

As we pulled into the driveway, I wondered if Aria was still up and what she and David would think of each other. As sneaky as he seemed to be, they might just find a way to hightail it out of here together. Either way, Dad was going to have his hands full.

I was still thinking about my conversation with Aria nearly four days ago, and I rather wanted to try to have another conversation with her, just to see if I could dig down to the root of what was happening. David and I were getting home a lot later than we'd planned, and darkness had fully fallen just as we'd hit the edge of Atlanta.

"This is where you live?" David's eyes were wide in surprise as he looked at the house.

"This is where *we* live. Remember what that security guard said. Don't screw it up."

He seemed to think about that as I pulled my suitcase out of the boot and headed for the door. He followed with his backpack, straining to see the edges of the house in the dim light.

I unlocked the door and stepped into the front hall. "We're here!" The tingle of the wards gave my skin a familiar prickle. If David noticed, he didn't say anything.

I was met at first with silence. Then I heard rummaging from Dad's suite on the far left side of the house. I gestured at David to follow, and walked through the foyer, past the formal living room, and into the kitchen/family room area. Dad emerged from the door that led to the owner's suite and smiled. It wasn't his usual smile, though. He was clearly upset and putting on a show of welcome. His third-eye chakra was wavering, fading in and out, and I knew something had happened in my absence.

"David, my boy, welcome. How was the journey?"

"Yeah, it was cool. I question Zora's musical taste, but that's my only complaint."

Dad chuckled, and it sounded hollow to my ears. "I've had the same complaint over the years." He paused there, like he was trying to decide what to say, and he refused to make eye contact with either of us. "It's been quite a stressful day, I'm afraid, and as much as I'd like to make snacks and have a chat with you two, I have a great deal yet to do before tomorrow. Zora, will you show young David around and allow him to select a room so he can get comfortable? I'm afraid I'll be wrapped up in work until mid-day tomorrow."

"Yeah, Dad, no worries." I kept my voice light, but I was itching to find out what was up. *Why hadn't Aria come down to meet David? More importantly, why hadn't Dad made her come down?*

"Thank you, my dear. I can't imagine what I'd do without you. David, I do look forward to catching up with you tomorrow. Again, I apologize for my abrupt greeting and departure. We'll do something fun tomorrow to make up for it, yes?" He reached out to shake David's hand, and held onto it for just a minute as a sign of affection.

"Hey, it's cool. I'm sure I can entertain myself around here!" David's eyes wandered over the large kitchen and big-screen TV. "Did you say I can choose my room?"

"Yes, indeed. We have several upstairs. You may have any room ... except Zora's, of course."

Wait, what? What happened to Aria?

David grinned, putting on all the charm, and Dad smiled back, a real one this time. "Awesome."

"Alright then, you two, I shall join you for lunch. You can choose the restaurant. The sky's the limit!" Then he turned on his heel and scurried back into his suite, closing the door behind him.

David turned to me with a raised eyebrow. "Not exactly what I expected, but whatevs. Can I pick my room now? And then maybe eat something?"

"Yeah, sure," I agreed, distracted and disturbed. "There are snacks in that basket on the counter, and you can help yourself to anything else you can find. Nosh yourself into a coma. The bedrooms are up here." I pointed to the stairway that led up to the second-floor landing and the row of six doors that made up that story. "That one is my room." I pointed to the one on the far right. "The middle one there is a bathroom, but a couple of the bedrooms have an en suite."

He didn't even wait for me to finish the sentence before he was bounding up two steps at a time. I followed, but more slowly. He had run down to the far left bedroom and flipped the light on. "Gotta vibe check each one," he announced, and at that moment, I didn't even care if he meant that figuratively or if it was one of his powers.

I rolled my suitcase into my room and surveyed my space carefully. I saw exactly what I'd expected to see: my bedside table drawer was ajar, and I was willing to bet that Aria's phone was gone. A quick check verified my suspicions. I wheeled around and headed for her room, only to find David standing in the doorway, a very curious expression on his face.

"This one," he said. "This one's my room."

"Are you sure?"

"Yep, I'm sure. There's energy in this room." His eyes were scanning the walls and the doorway to the en suite. For once he looked very serious. "I'm not sure what it is. But I'm going to find out."

"Maybe it's a ghost," I offered, hoping to lighten the mood.

"No," he replied, a little too quickly. "I know what ghosts feel like. This is something ... different."

I left him to settle in and went back to my room. I didn't like how all of this was shaping up. I knew Dad had said he had "work to do", but I suspected he was actually dealing with fallout of whatever had happened that left that bedroom vacant. Under normal circumstances, I was fine with the disappearing-aloof-father trick, but this time was different. I needed at least some answers about what was happening. If he didn't want to talk, maybe he'd at least answer a text.

Dad, I know you said you were busy, but where is Aria? What happened?

Several minutes passed by and then the blinking three dots appeared in the text string.

We had a bit of a disagreement, so I sent her back to Virginia.

I didn't need to see his chakras to be aware that I wasn't getting the whole truth. **Why would you do that? I thought we needed her for the planetary alignment?** For the past two years, Dad had been talking about the upcoming planetary alignment and how it would allow him to merge the powers of the Arcana and create a whole new legacy, and that was why we were tracking down all my half-siblings.

We will figure out another way. That's what I'm working on. Let's talk about this later.

That was all I was going to wheedle out of him, most likely, so I sent back **OK**, and lay down on my bed to stare at the ceiling and have a think.

***

I reflected back to my childhood in Brixton, in the south of London. For most of the time, it had been just Mum and me in our flat in the red brick building with the white trim. When I was very young, I'd gone to primary school with the rest of the neighborhood children, but as I got older, Dad started coming around more, and he'd started arranging for me to have private tutors instead. He'd paid for all of it, of course.

Then, when Mum got sick, we moved from our lovely corner of London to Dad's country house in Lewes. His family had owned the land for generations, he said. At first, I was excited to move to the posh little village, because I'd only ever seen the Lewes Bonfire Night celebrations on the telly. Our family history stretched all the way back to the Gunpowder Plot itself, Dad said. I never did get to attend the chaotic night parade with burnt effigies and massive gatherings, though I did watch from my bedroom window as revelers made their way to the sites on the edge of town for the bonfires and the fireworks. I was forbidden to leave the house on November 5th for any reason ... Dad warned that it was the most dangerous night of the year.

I didn't miss my friends from Brixton because I didn't really have any, and I'd never been anywhere like the country house. It was enormous and white in front, with older brick parts in the back. It had six bedrooms and a small guest house at the back of the drive. Dad gave us our own rooms, and hired doctors and nurses to come and help Mum a couple of times a week. I was allowed to go anywhere on the property I wanted, and as long as I did well in my studies, I didn't have restrictions on bedtimes or how much time I was allowed to spend on PlayStation or streaming movies.

We had meals together.

We talked, we played games, we even had the most magical Christmases anyone's ever seen.

We were a *family.*

But despite all the medical resources, my mum—my *Ìyá*— kept getting sicker. When it became apparent that she wasn't going to get better, she took my hand and told me it was my time to become Strength.

"Zora, my dove, my time is short. We have things we must do before it becomes too late."

I never tired of listening to the musical Nigerian accent in her voice, and it broke my heart that I wouldn't be able to hear it for much longer. "Ìyá, no ..."

"Do not argue with me, daughter. There will be time for mourning, but there is no time for denial. You must assume your birthright and take the Strength card and bond with it. I must show you how to do this so that the process may not be disrupted."

"Disrupted? By who? Bàbá?"

"Maybe. He wants to unite the Arcana; you know this. But he may believe you are too young for your power. You are not. The Universe determines when you become what you are meant to be, and no one can take that from you unless you choose to relinquish it."

"I don't understand, Ìyá."

"I know, my child, but you must trust me and the deity who waits for you."

"Does Ọya not wait for me?" Ọya was the goddess of my mother's home-land, and the divine energy from whom she derived her powers of Strength.

"I am unsure. But we will find out in time. The deity that waits for you is the deity of Strength most aligned to your spirit. You must meditate as you have seen me do and wait for whomever comes."

Tears prickled my eyes. I had known that my mother's illness was going to claim her, but I wasn't ready. I would never be ready. She pulled the Strength card out from under her pillow and handed it to me. She had let me hold it many times, and I stared at the familiar image of a woman with wild hair riding a lion. This time, as I gazed at it, I could only see my mother's face in the drawing, not so much in the features, but in the fierceness of the eyes.

"Give me your finger, my love. I apologize that I must hurt you briefly, but the Card must know that your blood is my blood."

I cringed inwardly at the thought, but I obeyed and stretched out my finger. My mother picked up her favorite brooch, a silver chrysanthemum, and pricked my finger with the pin. A small droplet of blood welled up, but I did not cry out. My mother nodded in approval, and then guided my fingertip to the card, tracing a thin line of my blood down the center.

"Sit in the sunshine, daughter. Close your eyes and let the sun warm you."

I took the card and scooted next to the window, holding the card between my palms, as I'd seen her do.

"Now, my dearest one, I want you to picture yourself on a tiny island in the center of a lake. Fix every detail in your mind. Imagine that there is a walking bridge that leads to the mainland. Can you picture this?"

"Yes, Ìyá."

"Good. Now you must sit and wait. Describe to me every detail of your island until the words flow away from you. Then wait in silence and your deity will come."

I did as she told me and pictured myself on a small island, only a little larger than my mother's bedroom, and imagined sitting on a picnic table staring at a small wooden bridge that extended across the water to the mainland, which was mostly covered in a dense fog. I described the scene for my mother.

"Describe the trees to me while you are waiting," she instructed me.

I launched into details about the oaks around me, knotty and tall, and excellent for climbing. I described the dirt, thick and brown with patches of grass that managed to get enough sunlight to grow. I told my mother about the warm air, like early summer's first breath. I imagined my hand running over the rough bark, and as I began to describe the feeling, my words got lost and I forgot about the place where my body sat. Only the island existed.

I turned my attention to the bridge and saw a silhouette in the distant fog, growing more distinct as it moved toward me across the wooden planking. It was a woman's figure, to be sure, but one that was constantly shifting—one moment lithe like a dancer, and the next curvy like a great mother. Her hair was black as the deepest night, but her skin seemed to change colors as if there were rotating lights. One moment, a warm brown, the next, a vibrant blue, and then a pale green. She wore a sari of gold, and a great lioness padded behind her, more of a companion than a pet.

Her dark eyes were fixed on mine.

"I did not expect one so young to call to me," she said simply, and it wasn't one voice, but many in a great chorus. I wasn't sure if I should apologize for my age or not.

"My mother is dying." I was surprised that I was able to say it without falling apart. "I am to become Strength."

"Indeed. And you call me to serve you?"

I felt like it was a trick question. "No, not to serve me. Guide me, maybe? I ... I'm not sure how this works. You are not my mother's goddess."

"I am, and I am not. We are all facets of the same jewel. Even I am not bound by one form, though you could have chosen any one of my faces to greet you."

"I don't understand." I was getting nervous. What was I doing? I was only 12, not old enough to be Strength. How could my mother die and leave this to me?

"You are filled with fears, small one," said the goddess' green face.

I nodded. "Strength shouldn't be afraid."

She shimmered, and then the blue face, wild and dangerous, regarded me. "Everything living knows fear. Strength and fear are not enemies."

I did not know what to say to her. The lion slipped from behind her and sniffed my arm, chuffing back to the goddess-of-many-faces.

The brown face addressed me next. "I am Jai Bhagavati Shri Maa Adishakti Durga Jagat Janani Jagdamba Parmeshwari Mata Rani, but you can call me Shakti. I am the essence of Woman and all Her strength. I greet you, Zora."

Somehow having a name for her made me feel better. "I greet you, Shakti."

She nodded at me and turned toward the bridge. "We will speak again. For now, attend your mother and embrace what remains."

When I opened my eyes again, the sun in my mother's room had shifted, telling me that much more time than I expected had passed. My mother was sleeping with a gentle smile on her face that I had never seen before.

Chapter 4

The next morning, I awoke at half-eight, and since Dad's and David's doors were still closed, I decided to go for a run. I jogged out of the driveway and up to where our residential street joined with Highway 41 and cut across at the light. At the outer edge of a church parking lot, I spotted a brown and orange Ford conversion van with a white high-top that looked like it had been around since the 1980s.

Sort of an unusual vehicle for our neighborhood, I thought to myself. Stranger still that it was at the outer edge of a church lot on a weekday, facing the road. *I wonder if someone used the megachurch as a campground last night?*

I was almost amused by the thought, but then the Jiminy Cricket voice in my brain started in on me again. *If Lia had been more careful about suspicious vans, you wouldn't have been able to kidnap her.* I ground my teeth and started to increase speed so I could sprint by the van. Just as I passed, the driver (who had apparently been reclined—probably sleeping—in the front seat) sat up and our eyes locked. He looked to be roughly my age, with tawny skin and dusty, shaggy hair. He gave me a familiar nod and smile as if we were old friends spotting each other across a crowded room. My skin prickled with energy and I put on a burst of speed. I was not, in a cruel twist of irony, going to be pulled into a kidnap van by some 20-something dosser.

I cut across the parking lot in front of the huge brick building and ducked into some tree cover, determined to zig-zag through side streets and gardens if I had to in order to make my way back home without him being able to follow. Either my plan worked, or I was totally bonkers, because I didn't see any sign of the van along my route back. Coming in through the side yard, I peeked out into our driveway before letting myself in through the garage door.

I felt like an idiot, and cursed myself for having kittens over some old banger of a vehicle in the car park up the street. My conscience was turning me into a complete plonker. Why in the world would I assume that he was after me? Some hobo decided to park his van in a church lot to have a good night's sleep out of the way of police interference, and somehow I'd made it all about me. I was losing it.

I slipped up to my room and stripped off my sweaty clothes; then I turned the shower water on as hot as I could stand it and stood underneath, letting the steam relax my lungs. I did box breaths to bring down my heart rate. It wasn't like me to be so paranoid and jumpy. What in the world was going on with me?

At 11:00, I decided David had had quite enough of a lie-in, so I went and knocked on his door. He didn't answer, so I knocked a few more times and then opened it up a crack. Sure enough, he was still knocked out, with ear buds in his ears assuring that he wouldn't have heard a meteor if it struck the house. I smacked his foot with the back of my hand and he sat bolt upright as if he'd been electrocuted.

"What the—"

I pointed at my ears, and after taking a second to orient himself, he pulled the buds out. "Good morning, Sleeping Beauty. It's 11:00. I suggest you drag yourself out of bed and take a shower. Dad's going to want to go to lunch soon."

"He said noon, right?"

"Yes, but it's lunch, not a doctor's appointment. He might be ready to go earlier."

"Whatever. Come get me in 30 minutes, okay? I don't need a whole hour."

I debated whether to drag him out of bed or give him his extra 30. Against my better judgement, I opted for choice B. "Alright, 30 minutes, but no more than that. You've already slept like 12 hours."

"Yeah, okay, Mom." He flipped over on his side and pulled his pillow around his head. I was almost looking forward to what would happen if he pulled this act with Dad. I walked out of the room without closing the door. Petty, yes. No regrets.

When I went back up to rouse him later, he was already up and in the shower. A few minutes later, he was downstairs wearing one of his new outfits and carrying his backpack.

"You planning on going somewhere?" I wiggled my brows at his pack.

"Never can be sure," he answered. "I've learned that it's wiser to keep all my stuff with me just in case."

That struck a chord. Poor kid. Yeah, he was annoying, but most 13-year-olds are. And most of his less-desirable qualities might be relics of having been in foster care for two years and even his less-than-optimal earlier years. Lack of trust was pretty common, particularly in older foster kids. Maybe I had judged him too harshly.

Dad's door opened with a soft chafing of wood. "Good morning, you two, though only barely. David, how did you sleep?"

"Horizontally." There was that grin again.

Dad chuckled. "Very clever. Zora, how about you?"

"Yeah, fine. Good to be home and in my own bed. You get on alright?"

"I did, thanks. I was up quite late working and researching, but I still managed a good seven hours. Have you all decided what you'd like for lunch?"

"How about barbecue?" David's eyes brightened up.

"Barbecue it is," Dad agreed. "I know a place not too far from here." And so we piled into Dad's silver SUV, and I let David sit up front. It sort of chapped me, if I'm being honest, but I didn't want to predict what would happen if yet another one of Dad's kids turned on him. Dad was mad enough when he couldn't bring Lia home; I imagine he was really sore about Aria being gone. I desperately wanted to ask about it, but that conversation would have to wait for another time.

The place we ended up was exactly what American barbecue places should be—with a comical amount of wood paneling and decent food served in disposable paper trays. David looked like he was ready to propose marriage to his full slab of baby back ribs.

"So," he asked, his mouth full of potato salad, "now that you've tracked me down and got me here, what's the end game?"

Dad and I were both caught off guard. "Direct and to the point," Dad said with approval. "I like that. Quite refreshing. The end game, dear boy, is that now that you're here with us, you can learn to use your unique skills to their full potential. I'm sure your mother, rest her soul, would have made sure you had appropriate training if she could have. As your father, I believe it's my duty to help."

"Uh-huh." David bit slowly into a rib and chewed before elaborating. "That's cool and everything, but how did you find out she even died? How did you know to look for me at all?"

"A very smart question. The truth is that I did check in with your mother periodically to see if she needed anything, and usually she told me to go to Hell. She never changed her number, though. I think she rather liked telling me to sod off."

"That sounds like her."

"When I wasn't able to reach her about a year ago, I became concerned and eventually hired an investigator. I was deeply distressed to hear of her passing, and immediately started searching for you."

"Do you always stalk your exes like that?"

"Only the ones who've borne my children." It was maybe the most brutally honest answer I'd ever known Dad to give. Even David was taken aback and wasn't sure how to respond right away. I suspected that was sort of Dad's gambit.

"Okay, so like, you've got a bunch of kids all over the place?" The tone in David's voice was more confusion than disrespect.

"I have a few. You have two other sisters besides Zora."

"And where are they? Are they Arcana, too?"

"One lives in Florida, and one lives in Virginia. And yes, Lia is the Moon, and Aria is Judgement."

Tension tightened Dad's voice. He was trying to be very open and accommodating, but underneath that thrummed his frustration that our siblings were in other states.

"When do I get to meet them?" David was pushing gently, and I think he sensed the exposed nerve he was poking. Like a dog with a bone, that kid.

"I couldn't really say. Aria visited recently, but I haven't really arranged for them to come for a big family reunion yet."

David's eyes glazed over for a second, then cleared. His third eye and heart chakras pulsed briefly. "Aria stayed in my room, didn't she?"

That earned him a raised eyebrow from Dad, and something like hope flashed across our father's face. "Why yes, in fact. How did you know that?"

"I get impressions of power sometimes. I felt power in my room. Like god power, not people power."

"Fascinating!" Dad was really on the hook now. I wish I had gotten a chance to warn him about how good David was at tugging on that line. "Tell me more about your abilities, David!"

"Well, I can charm people, make them like me. I can make them believe things or do things sometimes. And I can feel power. I can glamour myself to look like someone else my size."

"Marvelous! Did Zora tell you that we have a training facility where you can practice and sharpen your skills?"

Now it was David's turn to be surprised. "She did *not* mention that!" He shot me a reproachful side eye. "When can we go?"

Dad looked delighted. "There's no reason we couldn't go later this afternoon if that's what you want. I'm thrilled that you're so eager to learn."

"I want to make fire."

I almost choked on my Sprite. Of course that was what he wanted. But Dad took it in stride.

"Fire, you say? Now that's a new one. Have you made fire before?"

"No, but Mom could."

Dad just shook his head, grinning. I could tell he felt like his luck was turning, but something in me told me that it wasn't going to be the walk in the park he was envisioning. That would be a conversation for later, though. For the moment, everyone was getting on nicely, and there was barbecue. What more could a girl want?

Chapter 5

David spent two hours in the elemental practice station trying to make fire. It was a complete waste of an afternoon.

"Dad, it's not going to work," I told him as we sat in the observation room, watching the kid fail over and over. "I sat with him for 20 minutes, and no matter what he does or how hard he concentrates, his solar plexus does literally nothing when he works with fire."

"I know, I know, Zora. I don't feel the slightest power push when he works with elements. But for today, it doesn't matter. Let him enjoy himself."

"He's just going to get frustrated."

"With fire, yes, but once he starts to understand what skills he *does* have, that will pass."

"He's got a pretty good handle on his skillset," I remarked. "And no compunction about using it for petty personal gain either."

"Ah, well, let's not begrudge him that. Clean slate, yes?"

I paused, bracing to tread on thin ice. "Dad, what happened to Aria? You went to so much trouble to get her here, why did you just send her back?"

I could tell he was trying to decide how much of the truth to tell me. "She has the power of Judgement, Zora. She threatened to use it against me if I didn't let her return home. That same power cursed the Sheffield family for generations. I couldn't take that risk."

"Will two of us be enough? When the planetary alignment comes, I mean."

"The ritual to reunite the Cards we assemble will work no matter how many or how few we have. But I've put 20-odd years of my life into this plan to bring the Arcana back together, at least in part. Seems a shame to only unite three cards when there are two more out there connected to us. I will find a way to unite our blood. It's not even entirely clear that all the participants have to be willing."

Something in the way he said it chilled me. "What do you mean by that?"

"Nothing so nefarious as you're thinking by the look on your face, my girl. I simply mean that even if Lia and Aria don't voluntarily participate in the ceremony, my blood in their veins may still be enough to unite the Cards and their power. I've been researching the texts left behind by my father and his father before him, and the Cards operate via life force in the blood. It's not clear whether that has anything to do with someone's choice."

"So you're saying that whether they're here or not, it might still work?"

"Well, that part I'm unclear on. They may still need to be present."

I gave him a hard look. "There's no way you're going to get either of them to just pop round for a visit."

"No, that's definitely true, and there's the rub. I'm open to suggestions."

"I don't know, but I'll tell you what I'm *not* open to: More kidnapping. I'm not a fan. My conscience has been winge-ing at me for days."

"Noted, my dear. And I seriously doubt that would even be possible now, since they know us both. I'm trying to think of a way to get them here willingly, with the assurance that they are free to leave afterwards."

"Good luck with that."

"I appreciate your support, but not your snark." I was definitely poking the bear, as Americans liked to say. "At least David seems to be excited to be part of our little family."

"Maybe we should have tried harder to win Lia and Aria over rather than …"

"No more dwelling on the past, Zora. We must problem-solve for the future. I've been brainstorming ideas to activate their blood magic without them present."

"Wouldn't their Cards need to be here, too?"

"Perhaps, perhaps not. Since they have stepped into their roles as Arcana, the magic in their blood is active. You might say that the Card is a mere talisman at this point. The magic is within the person, not the paper. That is why the Cards follow their holders, I believe."

My brain was starting to hurt, and Jiminy Cricket was just waiting to have a go. I could feel him preparing to tell me a little something about myself.

David finally got weary of his failed efforts. We could tell because he threw the lit candle across the cubicle, probably hoping it would set something ablaze and give physical form to his frustrations. Fortunately, the weak flame blew out as it sailed through the air. The only damage was the wax drippings now littering the floor and wall of the work station, and David's wounded pride that he couldn't even make fire with a burning candle.

***

We stopped on the way back to the house to pick up the dogs, Tess and Darcy, who had been living the sweet life at a pet resort since we'd gone to Virginia to get Aria. The folks at Pet Paradise were sad to see them go because they were so well-behaved, which was largely because of the training school they'd been through when we first got them. I had to admit that I'd missed the knuckleheads.

David was overjoyed at the idea of having dogs, and they seemed to take to him pretty quickly, which I guess wasn't surprising since the kid had a canine deity. When we finally got home, Dad headed inside and I invited David on a walk to see the neighborhood. It seemed to me that if you'd had a sort of unstable life, you might like to have a good sense of your surroundings. Besides, the dogs needed some exercise.

"Yeah, okay," he responded, less-than-enthusiastically, "but can I play video games later? I saw that you had a really sweet set-up in the basement."

"I think that'd probably be fine." Instead of wandering down toward 41, I headed north into more of the residential area. "Sorry you didn't have any luck with the fire. I'm going to be honest with you, I can see in your chakras if you're using any magic, and you just weren't today. I don't think that's one of your skills, mate."

"I asked Coyote if I could make fire and He said, 'you can try!' I think He was jacking with me." He sounded resigned and disappointed. "I hate when He does that."

"Does He do that to you often?"

"Eh, sometimes. I think He thinks it's funny."

"That seems a little mean."

"I guess. But mostly, I think He wants me to learn things for myself instead of asking Him all the time."

I nodded. That actually seemed like it made some sense. Shakti was that way, too. But usually She just left me with some cryptic proverb or something rather than a direct answer. It amounted to the same thing, though. The doggos stopped to sniff around the edge of some woods and take care of their business.

"Can I ask you a question?" The kid seemed uncharacteristically serious. That might actually be a redeeming sign.

"Of course. I may not have an answer, and it might not be the answer you want if I do. But you can ask."

"That's fair. How long have you lived with him?"

"Dad? Since I was a little younger than you. Eight years. And he was around off and on even before that. I don't remember a life where I didn't know him."

"Don't you think it's weird that he was out there knocking up a bunch of Arcana women? I mean, that's weird, right?"

"It may seem that way, but he had a bigger purpose. You know how the Arcana are all split up?" David nodded. "Well, they weren't always that way. The Deck used to be united. People like us worked as a team. We used our different powers as one body to try and help keep the world on track."

"What does that mean, exactly?" We started walking again, and I was grateful that I didn't have need of the plastic bags I'd brought along to clean up after the pups.

"Well, we all have different powers, yeah? You can glamour. I can increase my physical strength for short periods of time. You and Dad can both direct people's thoughts. Other Arcana can get glimpses of the future. Working together ..."

"No, I mean, what does it mean to *keep the world on track*? Who decides what track is the right one?"

It was a question that had never occurred to me. "I don't know. I guess they'd all discuss it. Like a committee."

"What if normies don't like what the committee chooses?"

Another thing I'd never thought about. It all sounded so reasonable when Dad explained it, I'd never even questioned it. "I guess I don't know. It's been hundreds of years since the Arcana has been united."

"Maybe they split it up for a reason."

Ah, this one I had an answer for. "Yeah, well, the way the family archives tell it, there was a huge uprising against people perceived as witches back in the 1600's in Europe. The decision was made to scatter the Arcana so that they couldn't be exterminated."

"Maybe people rose up against them because they found out they were being mind-controlled and stuff."

"You think a lot of deep thoughts for a kid. Do you always pick apart everything people say to you?"

He stopped walking and looked me straight in the eye.

"If you don't do that, you can't protect yourself. You have to be suspicious of everything, Zora. Maybe you grew up kinda sheltered or something, but on the streets, people always want something from you. They always have an angle. And if you don't pick everything apart, you won't realize what they're up to until it's too late."

I put my hands on my hips, and Tess and Darcy stepped beside me, curious at this pause in their daily constitutional. "Okay, it's a fair point. But you do realize you're being a hypocrite, right? You mind control people. You manipulate people for your own gain. And you feel absolutely no guilt about it whatsoever."

He considered this, and didn't even seem offended. "Touché. But that really just proves my point, doesn't it?"

I had to admit that he was totally right.

Chapter 6

Sometimes I hate being right.

After that first day of enthusiasm on David's part, the itch to go train and test his powers took a sharp downturn. He turned into a very typical teenager, something Dad knew very little about.

David would sleep till 11, and then be grouchy when we got him up. When Dad would encourage him to go train, David would grumble about already knowing how to use his abilities. It seems that if he couldn't make fire, he was content with what he already knew.

"Why do I need to train if I already know how?" he complained.

"So that your skills will be finely honed, and so you can test yourself to see what else you might have the ability to learn." Dad was trying to be patient, but the planetary alignment was just a couple of weeks away, and he still hadn't figured out how to get the girls to come back. It was a right mess.

"I don't feel like it. Maybe tomorrow."

"Maybe today." Dad's voice was tight, and when I looked across the kitchen at him, his solar plexus chakra was glowing. *Uh-oh. He's trying to mind-push David.* I'd seen no indication that the wards and power dampening field were actually working on him, so I wondered if he'd sense what Dad was doing. He did, sure enough.

"Did you just try to mind-control me?" David looked at Dad through narrowed eyes. "That is so not cool."

"You're being difficult," Dad said simply. "You can't blame me for trying."

"Oh, I think I can."

I could see this building into a proper row if I didn't step in. "Alright, boys, play nice. How about we make a deal? David, you come with me to the training site and I'll run the battery of tests that shows where else you might have abilities. Then you get to pick what we have for dinner. Dad, you'll stay here and just trust me to take care of it. Yeah? Good?"

"You can't make me do anything," David insisted, his eyes still locked with Dad's. Darcy was zonked by the windows, but Tess was watching this back and forth like she was sitting at a tennis match.

"You are absolutely right. That's why I'm bribing you with food." I reached out a tendril of energy from my heart chakra and poked him with it. His eyes darted to me. "That's me tapping you with my energy. You're too far away for me to poke with my finger, and I don't have anything to throw at you."

His eyes twinkled slightly. "See?" he said to Dad. "That's how to be respectful. I haven't tried mind-controlling you, so you shouldn't do it to me, either."

"I am not susceptible to control. It appears you inherited that trait, or that it's part of your skills as the Devil. You're certainly living up to your title today, but I will agree to Zora's plan. Well negotiated, my girl. I will see you all at dinner time." And then he turned on his heel and retreated to the owner's suite side of the house, the dogs jumping up and following at his heels. There was a slight pause and then he slammed the door behind him.

David turned to me and crossed his arms.

"Don't turn that look on me, kid. We made a deal." I chuckled to let him know there were no hard feelings. He pouted at me for a minute longer, then grinned himself.

"Yeah, alright."

***

We spent about two hours in the lab, going through the same tests I'd done with Aria only ten days before. It seemed like so much longer. We'd already ruled out elemental skills, so I tried him on prognostication, telepathy, astral travel, telekinesis, and energy manipulation. Most were a bust, but telepathy and astral travel did show some promise. He very much liked the idea of being able to tell what people were thinking, and given his tendency to use his powers to satisfy his immediate wishes, I felt like that could be pretty dangerous. I didn't tell him that, though.

My read on his chakras also told me that his powers of mind control were different from Dad's, but that someday, they might be just as strong. The problem I had was that I wasn't about to drop my defenses to let him practice on me, and we didn't really have anyone else.

"So listen," I began. "You said you can make people do what you want them to *sometimes*. Is there any pattern to it as far as you can tell?" Maybe I could root out the differences just by asking the right questions.

He thought about it. "Well, I guess if they really kind of want to do it anyway, but think they shouldn't, then I can make them forget that they shouldn't. Kind of."

"Give me an example."

"Okay, so like, this one time I was on the subway, right? And this girl is all *blah, blah, blah* to her boyfriend, and it was super annoying. But he was just letting her talk, even though you could *totally* tell he didn't care about what she was saying at all. So I thought real hard at him to tell her to shut up. And then, like, out of nowhere, he looked up from his phone and yelled at her to shut up! Really yelled at her. Then he went back on his phone. She did shut up, though. I did the whole car a favor."

"You're a real Good Samaritan."

"Look, he obviously really wanted to tell her anyway. And one time, I made a guy run away. His friends wanted us to fight, but the guy didn't really want to. He just felt like he had to, you know, so his boys wouldn't think he was weak."

"How do you know he didn't want to?"

"I don't know exactly. Sometimes I can just feel what people really want. And he was really scared to fight. So I made him run. One of his friends sucker-punched me, though. So I tried to make one of the other guys hit him, but it didn't work."

"Because he really didn't want to." So David could make people give in to their desires. That was pretty on-brand for a Devil, honestly.

"Yeah. Are we done now?"

"I guess so. But listen, try not to be so difficult, right? Dad's temper isn't all that nice, and he's under a lot of pressure to make this ritual thing work. He's been building toward it for literally decades."

"I still wonder why though. Like what would be gained by even five of us uniting?"

"Well, I ..." I realized that that was yet another thing I hadn't considered.

"And what if this thing nerfs our powers by making us share? Or what if he's just trying to steal our powers?"

"You really have trust issues."

"So do you," he retorted. "You trust him too much. Is it just 'cause he's your dad?"

"He's yours, too," I countered.

"Nah, he's my sperm donor. He doesn't really care about me. It's all about this ritual thing. He needs me to be in on it. The question I've got is, *what's in it for me?*"

"Is that always at the heart of it for you? No thoughts about being part of something bigger?"

"Like what, *a family*? I never lived no Hallmark life, Zora, and I doubt I ever will. I gotta look out for myself. First law of survival."

"That's pretty glass-half-empty for a 13-year-old."

"Maybe it is. But you're pretty foolish for a 19-year-old."

"I beg your pardon?"

"I don't mean that in an insulting way. You just believe whatever he tells you. Have you ever stopped to ask *what's in it for you*? I bet you haven't. I bet you haven't asked a lot of things."

I was decidedly uncomfortable with the truth bombs he was dropping. "Alright, look, we're done for the day, like you said. What do you want for dinner? I promised you your choice."

"Fine. Change the subject, but you know I'm right. And I want pizza. Not some rotten chain, either. New York style pizza. REAL pizza."

I shook my head and grabbed my car keys. "You Google it, and we'll go get it." We walked out of the aluminum building and I locked the door behind us, distracted by the thoughts swirling around in my mind. We got in the car and I shifted into reverse. It was just then that I saw it in my rearview mirror.

A brown Ford conversion van with a white high top.

Chapter 7

Something must have shown in my face because David dropped his voice and said, "I sense it, too."

My eyes darted to him. "What do you sense?"

"Power. It's close."

"Can you tell where?" I was wondering if he could pinpoint it to the van.

He shrugged. "I'm not sure. If it were too far away, I wouldn't feel it. Maybe somewhere in one of the other warehouses?"

"How about that brown van over there across the lot?" It was partially obscured, but not exactly hidden.

"Yeah, could be. Should we go over there?"

"Not yet. It's too isolated here. Let's go to the pizza place and see if he follows."

We backed out and David identified a pizza place that looked acceptable that wasn't too far away. I followed the GPS directions, and 15 minutes later, we stepped out of the car and through the doors of the eatery, the smell of fresh-baked bread, garlic, and tomato wafting up our nostrils.

The van pulled into the convenience store in the adjoining parking lot.

"Alright, look," I told David. "I'm going to go over there and talk to the guy. What are the odds you'll stay here and call Dad if I need back-up?"

"But what if you need me?"

"We're in a very public place. Whoever he is, he probably won't try anything. But if something does go down, I need you to get Dad. When I go over there, I'm going to text you a picture of the license plate, and a picture of the guy if I can. Then, if you don't hear from me in three minutes, you call Dad and tell him where we are. Then if you want to come save me, you can. Can you do that for me?" I looked at him very intently, hoping he wouldn't be a total knob about it.

"You aren't going to try and bribe me?"

"No. I just need you to do this. Please."

I think it was the *please* that got to him. "Okay. Three minutes from the time you get over there. Can I order the pizza?"

"What? Oh, yeah, okay." I handed him some bills from my pocket. "Thank you. Three minutes."

I didn't even make an attempt to hide myself as I made a bee-line for the van. The driver spotted me halfway across the parking lot and stepped out of the vehicle to greet me. I snapped his picture and hit *send*, but couldn't get the license plate since I was facing the side of the van.

"Oy, what are you doin' following me?" I wasn't pulling any punches.

The man looked a bit surprised at my directness, but then an easy smile spread across his stubbly face, and a pair of the bluest eyes I've ever seen twinkled back at me. "Hello to you, too," he grinned, and I found my anger fading slightly. David's words of caution echoed in my ears, and I scanned the guy's aura for anything shifty. If he was another Arcana, I should be able to get some sense of his intentions. None of his chakras were active, which shouldn't have been possible if he was like us, but his aura swirled with magenta and white, a sign that there was nothing for me to fear from him, whoever he was.

"Who are you, and why are you following me?" I asked again, but less ragey this time.

"My name's Rhys Baker. I don't really know how to answer your second question."

"What is that supposed to mean?"

"It means literally that. I was just chilling in North Carolina, 'cause it's really nice this time of year, and then *BAM!* I felt like I needed to come to Atlanta. So I pulled up stakes and sort of ... well, it's complicated. But when I saw you in that church parking lot, I knew I was here to meet you."

"What kind of bollocks story is that?" My annoyance was back, not from fear, but from frustration at the nonsense he was spitting.

"Tell you what. Why don't you invite me to share that pizza with you and the kid, and I'll tell you all about it?" He flashed that disarming smile again, but there was no energy activity to show that he was trying to manipulate my free will in any way.

I stared at him for a second, then made a decision. "Alright, then, but we have to eat outside, and you have to stay downwind."

That earned me a hearty laugh. "Totally fair. I'm probably pretty ripe. I should've gone and showered at a truck stop yesterday. But I promise to go straight there once I'm nice and fed."

I rolled my eyes. "Come on." I started walking and I could hear him following me, whistling to himself as we walked. David's expression of total confusion was absolutely worth letting this strange homeless guy eat with us.

Inside, the clerk called David over to take his order. He looked over his shoulder at me, and I pointed at the picnic tables on the side of the building. He nodded, indicating he understood.

Rhys and I sat down at a table. "So," he began, "you didn't say what your name was."

"No, I did not."

"So untrusting," he teased me.

"I'm practicing," I replied curtly, but my rudeness was having no ill effect on his good humor.

"You're an Arcana, aren't you?" he asked, and I was grateful for David's heads-up that this guy had power, because I was getting no read on him whatsoever.

"I am. I assume you are, too?"

He stood and made a theatrical bow. "The Fool, at your service. And you are?"

"Untrusting, that's what."

"Ah, well," he sighed, sitting back down, "I suppose I'll have to earn your trust. Should I wait for the kid to get here with the pizza before I explain? He's one, too, right?"

"Yeah, he is." I thought for a minute. If I wasn't going to trust Rhys, I *definitely* should be careful about trusting David. He'd already shown hints of his colors, and I'd be wise not to ignore them. "I hate to be this way, but I think the less the kid knows, the better. He's ... troublesome."

Rhys considered this. "Okay, I'll give you the Cliff's Notes version, and you can decide what you want to do from there. But I will tell you this: This won't be the last time you see me, and it won't be because I'm following you."

"Is prediction one of your skills, then?"

"Sort of. More like insights, but they're never wrong. Like when I knew to come here. There is a great Pattern in the Universe that nudges us all along, and as The Fool, I have an instinctive knowledge of that Pattern. You and the kid and I are all connected."

"Are you talking about destiny? Fate? That sort of thing?"

"Not in the way that you mean. We all have the ability to make our own choices. We are more in balance when we follow the Pattern, but we don't have to."

"That sounds like a bunch of gobbledygook."

"You mean like a group of people with magic tarot cards and powers and direct connections to Divine Beings? That sort of gobbledygook?"

I couldn't help it. I smiled.

"Just that sort. My name's Zora. The kid is David."

"Nice to meet you, Zora. I'm not sure why I was drawn here, but it felt hella important."

My mind was racing. There was something so easy, so comfortable and familiar about Rhys, that I was inclined to trust him and believe that he was a friend, not a foe. But David's warnings were still fresh, and there was a strange wisdom in them.

"Okay, tell me this, and then I'll tell you what Arcana we are. Is that a fair trade?"

"You don't have to trade with me, Zora. I'll tell you what I can. Secrets are too much trouble for me. I don't live my life that way."

"So you just tell everyone you meet who and what you are?"

"It doesn't really come up. Only a handful of people would attach any meaning to the phrase *I'm an Arcana*, though I can think of more than a couple of people who would call me a fool. Little f, though." He grinned again, and it made me feel like we had an inside joke.

"Before David gets back, tell me why I can't read you. I should be able to sense when you're using powers, and not only can I not tell, it's like my senses are broken. I don't pick up anything from you." It truly bothered me that I couldn't even see his chakras at all.

"Oh, that's easy," he said. "The Fool is number zero in the deck. All powers are nullified on me. I can't be read, I can't be controlled, no one can see my future. That's my nature."

My jaw dropped. I wanted to ask more, but the door to the pizza place swung open and David came out with two boxes.

"Hey." He looked at Rhys. "'Sup?"

"Hey, yourself," Rhys smiled back. "I'm Rhys. And Zora tells me your name's David."

David looked back and forth between the two of us. "You're one of us, right?"

"I am. I'm the Fool."

"Sucks for you, man."

Rhys erupted into laughter, and David and I found ourselves chuckling as well. "Nah, it doesn't suck. I lean into it."

"What's up with the *kidnap* van?" He stressed the word for my benefit.

"That's a rolling palace, my dude!"

David's eyes grew wide. "So you *live* in there?"

"Heck, yeah! I wouldn't have it any other way. I go where I want, when I want. That's why I was able to come here at the drop of a hat." I shot Rhys a look, hoping he wouldn't go into any more detail in front of the kid.

"So you're, like, homeless?"

"No, my man! The whole world is my home. Priscilla there—that's my van—is my shelter and my ticket anywhere I want to go."

"I guess that might not be so bad. How do you eat, though?"

"With my mouth, mostly." That was such a David-like answer coming out of Rhys's mouth that we all ended up laughing. "Seriously, though, I'm tapped into the Universe, and sometimes I do readings or reiki healings on people. There are psychic fairs all over the country. So when I need a little scratch, I just sign up for one and earn some cash. Nothing fancy about it."

"Huh. That's cool, I guess. I'm the Devil."

"I'll just bet you are."

"I guess we have some stuff in common. We don't like being told what to do or how to do it. We're rebels. That's pretty dope."

"I guess I'm a rebel in a way. But mostly I just like being free. It's not about going against what others want. It's just wanting to follow wherever the adventure takes me."

"So, um, I'm Strength," I said abruptly.

"That seems pretty appropriate, actually," Rhys nodded.

"So why were you following us then?" David asked, biting into a slice of pepperoni and sausage pizza.

Rhys leaned back and crossed his arms. "Ah, that's the question, isn't it? To be honest, I don't even really know myself. I just felt drawn to Atlanta, and then I kept narrowing it down until I found you. Maybe I'm supposed to help you with something."

"Maybe he's supposed to be there for the planetary alignment thing. What do you think, Zora?"

I felt my back muscles tense. "Maybe." David might have accused me of being overly trusting, but with the details of Dad's plan? Definitely not. I wished I had telepathy as an ability so I could tell David to shut his gob.

"Planetary alignment, huh? That sounds pretty interesting. I like astronomy. I mean, I don't know that much about it, but I like looking at the stars when I'm way far out, away from cities and there's no light pollution."

I felt like I needed to distract him away from this line of conversation. He wasn't part of Dad's plans, and Dad didn't even know about him. The voices in my head started arguing again.

He's another Arcana ... he could be part of the Cards uniting, making up for Aria or Lia. What if the ritual does bind our powers? Would we want to be bound to him? He's not of our blood. Having him there might ruin the whole ritual. If David is right, and there are negative effects, would it be fair to pull in an unassuming stranger?

My mind was spinning.

"Look, Rhys, I'm not really sure how much we should tell you." The direct approach was probably best. "At least not yet. If you feel like we were meant to meet up, then you're probably right. But let's not just drop all our deepest, darkest secrets in our very first conversation, yeah?"

He nodded slowly, sizing me up. "Okay, I guess that's fair enough. Can I still have a slice of pizza?"

Chapter 8

I couldn't quite put my finger on it, but something was *different* after meeting Rhys. I hadn't actually met any other Arcana until meeting Lia last year, and I'd felt the same way then: like something in the Universe had shifted and a series of events had been put into motion. I'd felt it again the last time I saw Aria. Now this. Only two days had passed, yet I felt like we were all barrelling toward *something*.

David seemed different, too. Rhys's life of wandering and freedom had struck a chord, and the already petulant little snot was getting worse. I'd given up trying to reason with him. Bribery with food was a temporary solution. If he was going to fight Dad at each turn, I wasn't going to be able to run interference every single time.

Dad, for his part, was at a loss. He didn't know how to deal with someone who said *no* to him. He and David argued almost any time they spoke, and they were equally stubborn. Dad had straight-out forbidden me from driving David anywhere for any reason as long as he was being bratty. Since we had food and PlayStation, though, the kid hadn't even noticed yet. Probably didn't hurt that Tess had taken to plopping on the downstairs sofa beside him while he played.

Maybe it was David's admiration for Rhys's wanderlust that drove the kid to go on walkabout one evening without a word to either of us. I was watching anime on my laptop when Dad burst in the door, something he rarely did.

"Have you seen your brother?"

I hit pause on my video and looked up. Dad's hair was disheveled, as though he'd been running his fingers through it repeatedly. "No, not since I came in here; why?"

"He's not in his room or the basement, and his knapsack is missing."

I set the computer aside and headed for the kid's room. The bed was a wreck and food wrappers littered the bedside table and floor, but the backpack was nowhere to be found. I sighed.

"Last time I saw him was about an hour ago. Did you try texting him?"

"I tried calling, but he didn't pick up," Dad confirmed, his jaw set in frustration.

"Kids don't answer calls. You have to text. I'm sure it's nothing. I'll find him." I was trying to sound calm, but my gut was doing flip flops. Why would he take off without saying anything? Had he decided that he'd rather go it on his own and not be bound by Dad's rules? "Why don't you stay here in case he comes back, and I'll drive the neighborhood and keep trying to reach him?"

With a grim nod of his head, Dad stomped back downstairs, and I whipped out my phone to text David.

Hey, kid. Where r u? There was no reply, and I didn't relish the idea of Dad having another one of us disappear on him. Mostly, I didn't relish the thought of how pissed off he'd be. I backed to the end of the driveway and then thought to text Rhys.

Are you parked at the church?

The reply came a moment later. *Yeah, 'sup?*

Is David with u?

No. Everything ok?

Probably. He took off. I'm going to look 4 him.

Need help?

Sure, thx. I'll check the neighborhood. Will u check ur side of the street?

Will do.

I appreciated Rhys cutting my job in half, and as I backed out of the driveway, I tried to remember the path we'd walked when I showed him around. It was as good a place to start as any.

***

About twenty minutes later, I found the little git lying on a picnic table at a park a few blocks away. I jumped out of my car and slammed the door, not even bothering to turn off the ignition.

"Oi, kid, what's the big idea?"

He sat up on one elbow. "What? Can't a dude get some privacy?"

"You had us all worried. You grabbed all your gear and disappeared. Why didn't you tell me you were going out?"

"It's a free country," he shrugged, and I wanted to throttle him for his sass.

"Not when you're 13, it ain't. You at least need to tell someone where you're going. This is a safe neighborhood, but you don't know your way around."

"Aw, Zora, I had my cell. I could call you if I got lost."

"Yeah, well, you didn't answer any of your messages, so how were we to know you were okay?"

He looked sheepish for a moment. "It was in the bottom of my bag. I guess I didn't hear it buzz."

"Why'd you take all your stuff? Were you not planning on coming back?"

"'Course I was. I just always keep my stuff with me. Habit."

"Yeah, well, Dad's in a proper tizzy."

"So sweet that you all care so much." His cheekiness, while sometimes endearing, was doing my head in this time. This was Dad's fight, not mine.

"Come on, get in the car. And if you want to go for a stroll in future, let me know, yeah?"

He grinned and shrugged, then slid off the table and followed me to the car.

I texted Dad to let him know I'd found David, and also to give him a few minutes to gather himself so he didn't completely lose his head when we walked in the door.

As it was, Dad came out of his room long enough to give David a stern glare that would sour milk, then stormed off and slammed his bedroom door.

David opened his mouth to say something, but I interrupted him. "Look, just don't. Why don't you go grab a snack and play a game or something. I've had all the excitement I can take tonight."

"Yeah, okay. See you tomorrow."

I headed up the stairs toward my room.

"Hey, Zora?"

I stopped and turned around halfway. "Yeah?"

"Sorry I worried you."

I nodded and went back up to finish watching my video, but I had a hard time relaxing as my mind spun.

***

It was late at night, and I lay in my bed trying to contain the growing sense of unease. I'd considered trying to run it out of my system even given the late hour, but somehow, I knew that wouldn't work. And it wouldn't work because, despite the unrest in the house, the real reason I felt wrong was because of what was happening inside me, not what was happening with everyone else.

I was questioning everything. I had done some horrible things over the past year, things that weren't in character for me, except for the fact that I'd grown up being loyal and obedient to my father.

But *why*? Was he using mind control on me, or was I just that brainwashed? Maybe both. I didn't have the answers, I couldn't get the answers, and my whole vibe was out of balance.

I sat bolt upright. It was as though a door had creaked open that I had forgotten was even there.

How long had it been since I'd meditated?

How long had it been since I'd spoken to Shakti?

How long had it been since I'd even *thought* of speaking to Her?

A little over a year, that's how long. Since we first made plans to go to St. Augustine looking for Lia.

I pulled a chair over to the window and looked out at the waxing moon. I closed my eyes, steadied my breath. I pictured the island with the bridge, the picnic table and the trees, but everything was covered with a dense fog. My heart was pounding, but I forced my consciousness to this place and out of my bedroom in Atlanta.

"Shakti!" My voice was swallowed by the thick air around me.

Weak light illuminated the mist, and I had the sense that I wasn't alone, but I couldn't see more than a few feet in front of me. I searched for the words to invoke the Goddess, but my mind seemed as foggy as the island.

Of course it was. The island was a construct of my mind. Duh.

With this realization, the air around me grew lighter and I could see a few more inches in each direction.

"Shakti!" I called again. "How do I clear my mind?"

Mind ... mind ... mind, my voice echoed back.

"Right. It's my mind." I was on the edge of something. This was a puzzle I could solve if I stayed calm. "If it's mine, then I should be able to control it." The mists receded ever so slightly.

I waved my arms frantically, as if I could windmill the fog away. When that didn't work, I thought back to the comic books I used to read as a kid. I drew a deep breath and tried to blow the thickness out of the air like Superman with his super breath. Sadly, that didn't seem to have much effect either. How do you get rid of fog?

Though I could not see it, I could hear the water lapping softly against the edges of the island.

Water. It was a clue, I was sure. I started to move forward carefully, but the mists swirled around my feet and I feared what would happen if I fell in. I also couldn't tell where there might be rocks, roots, or other dangers. Instinctively, I reached for my back pocket where I kept my phone so I could try using the flashlight. Of course, there was no phone to be found in this mental-spiritual construct.

"Brilliant, Zora," I chastised myself. But the back of my mind itched like I had found another clue.

Light. Water. Fog. What would a ship at sea do?

A lighthouse. I needed to make a lighthouse.

A zing of realization electrified me. *I AM the lighthouse!* I felt like a bit of an idiot, but I felt my way along until I found the picnic table, and climbed up on top. Then I took a deep breath and released it slowly, pushing energy into my *muladhara*, my root chakra. I pictured it glowing a deep red at the base of my spine, its light reaching downward and creating a complex root system into the earth, stabilizing me as though I were one of the trees.

"I am connected to the Divine Mother and Her bounty," I said aloud. "From my roots come my strength, and I have no fear."

I felt the warmth of the *muladhara* spreading through me as I spoke the words. I had not invoked my chakras this way for years, but it felt like the thing to do.

I took a second breath, and exhaled glowing orange light into my *svad-histhana*, or sacral chakra. A rush of endorphins flooded my system, filling me with a sense of excitement and joy.

"I celebrate the Mother's gifts of creation. From this ecstasy of spirit comes my ability to find pleasure and inspiration in the world around me."

A third breath ... in and out. I poured golden energy into my *manipura*, the solar plexus chakra, right behind my belly button. I felt my aura vibrate with the power, like a car revving the engine.

"I embrace my power, my strength of self, and there is no force that can prevail over me if I remember the Divine Mother within me."

Another deep breath, but I was surprised at the feeling of discomfort as I pushed green energy into my *anahata*, or heart chakra. I knew I couldn't stop, though, so I pushed through the pain, imagining the light coming from within me and squeezing mud out of the center of my chest like toothpaste out of a tube. As the blockage cleared, I found myself awash with emotion, mostly deep sadness and loneliness and longing, and tears streamed down my cheeks.

"I honor my heart, and know that love is strength. The Divine Mother's love nourishes us all, and the reflection of that love in me is the essence of connection with all things." My voice cracked as I said the words, and even in the midst of the power, I knew I'd have to deal later with the repressed feelings I'd just cut loose.

I inhaled another shaky breath and lit up my *vishuddha*, or throat chakra in a deep blue.

"I thank you, Mother, for my voice, that I may speak the truth within me to others. With this gift, I can illuminate the darkness for those who are lost."

Almost there, but as I drew air in and tried to exhale power into my *ajna*, or third eye, I felt as though I was pushing against stone. On a spirit level, there was a definite blockage in my way. I took several slow, steady breaths, each time exhaling my power through my forehead with rich indigo light. I could feel it seeping around the edges, but the block stayed in place.

The thought flitted through my mind that my father might have placed it there to stop me from seeing the truth, but that seemed too simple an answer. The ache in my heart chakra told me that while he may have put it there, I had cemented it in place myself because I wanted to believe in my father's love.

The funny thing about the third eye is that it doesn't show you what you want to see, it shows you what's real. And knowing the truth often came with consequences, ones that my heart hadn't been willing to risk after I'd lost my mother.

I opened my palms, and with my next breath, I reached back down into my root chakra and pulled energy through all the others as I inhaled. I held my breath for a brief second, bracing myself for answers I did not want.

Then with all the spiritual force I could muster, I pushed the swirling, multicolored light from behind my eyes, screaming something that sounded an awful lot like a karate *kiai*. A sharp pain ripped through my head like a weed-whacker as the blockage exploded outward in rays of bluish-purple.

My knees threatened to buckle, but I pumped strength into the red roots holding me to the earth.

"I accept the truths revealed by my third eye and set aside the vanity that would tempt me into believing pretty lies. Shakti, my Great Mother, I beg you for clarity and the strength to trust my intuition." My voice was ragged and hoarse.

There was a soft *pop* above my head as my *sahasrara* (my crown chakra) sprung to life, radiating a soothing purple in all directions and pushing away the fog, revealing the island in all its greenery. Sunlight dappled along the ripples in the water, and a gentle breeze caressed my skin.

In the center of the bridge, a smiling woman with skin the dark blue of midnight regarded me with one of her many sets of arms crossed in front of her.

"Well, it's about time," she chuckled. "I've been waiting for you."

"Why was it so hard to find you?"

"Well, you've been gone for quite a while, I think. Time moves different-ly for me, but it seems like I haven't seen you in ages. And then there was all that interference." She made a face as if she'd smelled something rotty.

I felt bad that I hadn't meditated in so long, but I was more concerned about the fact that it hadn't even occurred to me for more than a year. "Sorry about that. I ... well, I don't know why I haven't come. And I don't know what the fog was."

"Don't you?" She eyed me critically, and three of her arms started pulling her hair into an elaborate bun.

"Not exactly. I think ..." I paused, not wanting to voice my suspicions, "I think maybe my father has been blocking my abilities."

"Oh, I don't think he can do that." She crossed the bridge and sat gracefully on the picnic bench. Two hands smoothed her silken red and gold saree and then folded themselves demurely in her lap. I sat across the table from her.

"He can't?"

"Well, not in the way that you mean. Your father is the Magician, and he is older than you are, but no Arcana is any more powerful than another. You just have different skills. He can't strip power from you, just as you can't strip it from him."

"But then why is my mind so mucked up? Why have I been going along with whatever he tells me and not questioning the morality or the consequences?"

"You may be Strength, Zora, but you are still human. And a young one at that. The Magician cannot strip you of power, but he can persuade you that you don't need to use it. Persuasion is one of his talents, I believe."

She was right. Dad's deity was Mercury, well-known for His eloquence and leadership. "So he didn't create the fog or the blockages in my chakras?"

"Oh, no, my dear. You did that yourself." Four of her arms widened into an elaborate shrug. This was an aspect of her I'd never seen, and to be honest, it was weirding me out a little. I'd seen her skin in different colors, I'd seen her with a lion, I'd even seen her with extra eyes. But ten arms, each seemingly with its own mind?

"Forgive me, Shakti, but um ..." I couldn't figure out how to ask about the extra limbs. "Which aspect of you am I seeing today?"

She smirked, and I could tell that she'd been wondering when I'd ask. "You've seen many of my faces, each time according to which part of me you needed. You choose my form when you call to me. This is as it is with women, yourself included. We are many faces in one, and our form changes when we need it to. Today you summoned me as Durga. I have fought demons in this form, among other things." Her arms fanned out into a great circle that reminded me of ancient art I'd seen in books. The fingers all snapped in unison, and suddenly, each hand was bearing a different weapon. Several more arms appeared as well and her eyes glinted with the promise of battle. "Do you have demons which need to be slain?"

I was a little unnerved by this version of Her. "I ... well, not demons, I guess ... and I don't know about any slaying ..."

"Oh, there are many kinds of demons. Some come from without, and some come from within. When you activated each of your chakras, you acknowledged a demon or two, I suspect."

She had me there. "I don't know what to do. I feel like I've lost myself, and what's worse, I feel like my father has been manipulating me, even using his powers against me."

"You are probably right." The fingers snapped again and the weapons disappeared. "What will you do about that?"

"Well, I'm not going to kidnap anyone anymore, that's for sure."

"A good start, but if you called me in a battle form, there is more in your heart than passive resistance."

My heart chakra pulsed, and new waves of aching pain surged through me. "What am I supposed to do? He's my father!"

"He is, and when you were young, he embraced that role, but he is many other things, too. You must see him for what he is with clarity. You must let your heart see what your third eye sees. Then you must choose to accept it, tolerate it, or reject it. The decision is yours."

I thought of the spiritual stone that had been blocking my third eye, stopping me from seeing the truth. I wanted to blame him for putting it there, but Shakti was right. I had blocked it myself so I could see him as my *bàbá*, not as a manipulative and power-hungry man who might be using me to gain for himself. The emptiness I had glimpsed before filled me.

Shakti reached across the table and took my hands in two of hers. Her eyes reflected the depths of the Universe, full of both empty space and life at the same time.

"You are not a little girl anymore, Zora. You are Strength, and it is time to take on your full mantle."

A tear escaped the corner of my eye, and I didn't bother to wipe it away. "My father is all I have. I ..."

"Is he?" she interrupted. "Or is that what you've been persuaded to believe? Zora, you must see the truth—all of it, the light and the dark—so that you can choose the right course of action. Peel away what you think you know. Ask questions, even hard ones, and do not settle for evasive answers. You cannot know your course if you cannot see it."

I thought of David. "Someone else gave me that same advice."

"Then isn't it about time you followed it?"

It was well after midnight when I woke fully from my meditation. Thoughts and fears swirled through my head, and though I knew I couldn't avoid a mental reckoning forever, I kept pushing them away. Couldn't I, just for one more night, pretend that my father was the same man who put up our Christmas tree in Lewes and wheeled my ailing mother in front of the hearth while we watched movies together and ate Maltesers?

Once the illusion was cracked, though, there was no way of repairing it. So I crawled into my bed and curled up fetal around my pillow and cried myself to sleep like I did the night my mother died.

Chapter 9

When I finally woke up, I had a splitting headache, and my whole face was swollen from crying. I could feel it even without looking. I looked at my smartwatch, and was surprised to find that it was nearly 10 a.m. The sun seemed to be slow getting started, too, because no bright light was beating against the blinds.

I dragged my carcass out of bed and went to look outside. The day looked like I felt: soggy and gray.

After a quick trip to the loo, I fixed my mind on the kettle downstairs. I'd start with some tea to try and get my brain working, then take the rest of it step by step.

I trudged out of my room, intent on the caffeine infusion only a cup of hot water away, but I stopped dead in my tracks as I passed David's room.

The door was closed like always, but there was a metal bar across it, screwed to the door about six inches above the knob. Tess was lying in front of the door with her head on her paws, looking forlorn. What was happening?

I spotted Dad sitting out on the screened porch behind the kitchen. Bypassing my tea for the moment, I headed straight for him.

"What is that thing across David's door?"

"Good morning, Sunshine," Dad greeted me, never looking up from the news he was reading on his tablet.

"Fine," I huffed, exasperated. "Good morning. What is that thing?"

"It's an emergency door barricade." He took a sip of his coffee, but still never looked up. "Do you know that he sleeps with those bloody earbuds in his ears? He never even woke up when I put the screws into the door."

"What are you barricading him from?"

"Think of it as being grounded. He refuses to hone his skills, and his continued belligerence makes him untrustworthy. Plus, lately, I think he's become a bit of a flight risk. So I can't take the chance that he'll make a run for it before the alignment next week."

My eyes widened in shock. "You locked him in his room? For a week?"

"Oh, don't be so dramatic. He has his own bathroom, and I put a huge pile of food in there before I put up the barricade. I'm not a monster."

My jaw hung open. He actually believed that what he was doing wasn't monstrous.

"Dad! Put down the tablet and talk to me about this!" Darcy came trotting around from the other side of the kitchen to stare at me. Apparently, he didn't like my tone.

Dad sighed dramatically, as if he were dealing with a hysterical teenager and it was all terribly inconvenient.

"Zora, don't overreact. I'm not going to hurt the boy, and in fact, he can continue to live his sleep-and-play-video-games life at my expense until he's 18 once all this is over if that's what he wants to do. But with your sisters already distant, I can't run the risk of another of my progeny disappearing before the alignment. I've worked too hard."

He made it sound so reasonable, and yesterday, I might have been tempted to rationalize it all away. Even now, my brain was trying. *It's better than life on the street ... the worst that will happen is that he'll be bored ...* But I knew better, and with my chakras cleared, I wasn't falling for my father's logic.

"There's no way he's going to stand for this, Dad. He'll find a way to get the police over here."

"Ah, very practical of you, my girl, but I thought of that. His room faces the woods, and I removed his computer and his phone before installing the barricade. You know he never even rolled over? That boy sleeps like the dead."

"So you're saying he doesn't even know what you've done?"

"Oh, I imagine he'll figure it out in a couple of hours when he wakes up and wants to head to the basement to play video games."

My mind was screaming, but I kept my face neutral. "What if he's in danger? How do we get him out?"

"Well, in the unlikely event that does happen—let's say he figures out how to start a fire after all—I have set the release crossbar in the next room. We can get to him in a matter of seconds if needs be. As I said, I'm not trying to harm the little cur, I'm just trying to keep him here for a few days."

I nodded, trying to look agreeable. I didn't want him to know that I wasn't under his sway anymore. Could he tell? Maybe.

"Are you sure he has enough food?"

"Should be more than enough, even if he is a teenage boy. Most of it is non-perishable, but I did put some apples and oranges in there for good measure."

"Wouldn't want him getting scurvy," I quipped.

Dad chuckled and went back to reading his tablet. I wandered back into the kitchen to get my tea and tried to plan my next steps while it was steeping. *What is it with Dad and kidnapping?* Obviously, I had to extract David and get him out of here. I wondered if I should reach out to Aria or Lia. There was quite literally bad blood between us, but now that my allegiances were shifting, maybe they and their other families could help.

I wasn't sure why, but I really wanted to talk to Rhys. He was as clear-headed a person as I'd ever met in my albeit sheltered life.

Once I finished my tea, I poked my head back out on the porch. Dad hadn't moved, and by the lack of ruckus, it was clear that David wasn't awake yet. "I think I'm going to go for a walk."

"No running today?"

"Nah, it's already in the 80's out there. I had a bit of a lie-in today. I think a walk would do me good, though. I didn't sleep too well."

"Alright, enjoy yourself. Take water with you."

I nodded and closed the porch door behind me and looked at my father through the glass panel. For just a moment, I flashed back to him sitting at the outdoor tea table in our garden in Lewes, reading a physical newspaper like he used to do sometimes when I was younger. I snapped a quick photo on my phone, wanting to hold onto that moment of nostalgia for as long as I could, even while I was seeing that version of my father slip away.

As I poured the water, I did a mental check of my chakras. All still open, though my heart chakra was hurting again. I had a feeling it would be for a while. Maybe forever.

Chapter 10

I headed toward the church parking lot, and sure enough, Rhys's van was parked in the shade. Van Morrison's "Brown-Eyed Girl" floated out of the cracked windows, and the engine was running. I walked around to the sliding door on the passenger side and knocked. There was a rustling inside, and then the door slid open.

"Hey, stranger!" Rhys greeted me, his eyes twinkling with amusement. "I had a feeling you were going to come looking for me today. You look ... different."

"I am, a bit. Up for a chat?"

"Yeah, always! Hop in! Where's the kid?"

"He's still sleeping, but ... well ..." I found myself hedging about spilling all of Dad's secrets; I'd been keeping them for so long. And what would Rhys think of me when he found out about my involvement in all of this? I looked nervously over my shoulder in the direction of the house.

He noticed my anxiety. "You want to drive a bit? I could use some gas and stuff ..."

"Yeah, let's. Could you go right on 41 instead of left?" I didn't want Dad noticing Priscilla. She was rather stand-outy.

Rhys shot me a little side-eye, but it was the curious type rather than the judgy type. "No problem. I'll drive, you talk."

As I slammed the door, I noted that the inside of the van smelled a bit like chicken tikka masala, and for a split second, I was back in London, eating at a hole-in-the-wall Indian place off Tottenham Court Road near the British Museum. My heart groused at me as I buckled into the passenger seat and prepared to spill my darkest secrets to someone I'd only known for a few days.

"Quick question before I start: Why do I feel the urge to trust you and tell you literally my whole life story? Is that one of your powers?" I didn't want to offend Rhys, but I thought it was time I started asking a LOT more questions. About everything.

He considered my question as he pulled out of the parking lot. "It's not an active ability, but Fools are non-judgemental by nature. We make really good listeners. You should meet my mom."

"She's still alive? How did you inherit the Card, then?" I realized how rough that sounded after it came out. "Sorry. That was harsh."

"It's cool. But I don't think anyone HAS to die, at least not with all the Cards. Sometimes a person doesn't want to be an Arcana anymore, like Mom."

"She didn't want to be the Fool anymore?"

He shrugged and smiled. "I mean, back in the day, she was all about adventure and *carpe diem*, you know? But she's in her 50's now, and she doesn't really want to do the RV life anymore. She's met a bunch of friends down in Florida, and moved into a really nice little bungalow in Cassadaga. There's a lot of psychics there and stuff, and a lot of people with that hippie vibe. But she kinda wanted to settle down, so when I turned 18, she gave The Fool to me. She sold the RV, bought her place, and bought Priscilla from some old dude who couldn't drive her anymore because of his eyesight or something. I go see her every few months or so."

"What about your dad?"

"I never knew my dad. I'm not even sure of his name. My mom hooked up with some guy at a music festival many moons ago, and she never saw him again. All I've ever known of my dad is a crusty Polaroid."

I was surprised at how cavalier he seemed about being the product of a one-night stand. I guess Fools truly were wired differently. "How old are you?"

"Almost twenty-three. I've been out on the road for about four years full time. It's a great life, but I can see how it might get old for some people."

"I don't think I could do that for very long," I confessed. "I don't think I've ever not had a home to go to."

"Home is what you make it. For me, Priscilla is home. My mom is home. Doesn't really matter what my coordinates are. And while I'm happy to tell you about my life, I don't think that's why you walked across the highway, is it?"

"No, I guess it's not. I've been thinking a lot about what you and David said about thinking more critically. I ..." It was so hard to say the words out loud. "I think my dad has been controlling me for years. Some of it may be his abilities as the Magician, some of it may be classic gaslighting, but I think a good bit of it has been good old-fashioned denial on my part."

"It's not just a river in Egypt," he smiled.

"What?"

"Denial. De Nile."

I smacked his arm. "I'm trying to talk to you here."

"Sorry. I couldn't help myself. Your dad's the Magician? So your mom must've been Strength, then. That's quite a power couple."

"It's complicated. Anyway, the long and the short of it is that after me, my dad had kids with a few other Arcana women, then he sort of settled down with us and I've been with him my whole life since. Pretty much just me and him since my mum died."

"I'm sorry for your loss. Your mom must have been a very open-minded person to be cool with ... you know. I guess he really has a type."

"Like I said, it's complicated. My mum was the only one who knew what he was."

"So David has a different mother than you, I take it."

"Yes. And I have two sisters: one in Virginia and one in Florida."

"Must make the holidays interesting."

The import of what I was trying to tell him just wasn't sinking in past those floppy curls of his. I was going to have to be more direct. "Look, my dad was intentionally having split-Arcana kids. The women, except for Mum, were sort of beside the point to him."

Rhys's jaw set, but he didn't say anything.

"I know how that sounds. It's terrible. Awful. And it's only just sinking in to me now *how* awful because I never thought too hard about it before. He was present in *my* life, so I didn't really care about the others until about a year ago when he started trying to find them."

He nodded slowly. "So ... why would he deliberately father other Arcana kids and then not be part of their lives? Finding another Arcana isn't exactly easy. You're literally only the third I've ever met in my whole life, counting my mom. We don't exactly have a social media page or anything."

"He does a lot of research. Genealogies, family trees. He's got massive amounts of records. As to why? He wants the Arcana to be united like it was back in the beginning. He wants to build a legacy."

"Okay. Why?"

"David asked me that, too. I don't completely understand it, if I'm honest. My father's family has records of the Magician all the way back to the beginning. Like 400 years, maybe more. I know that the Arcana were feared and in danger when witch trials were all the rage in Europe, and that's why they chose to scatter. I know that my father's family stayed in Lewes, near where it all began, and kept track of everyone for a while."

"Okay, so maybe he feels like everyone had to split up because the world wasn't ready, and now he feels they should reunite. There are other Arcana that might agree. So why not just go find those people rather than making double-dipped magical babies?"

"That's the part I don't really know. I always assumed it's because he thought it would guarantee a handful of people would be on his side. But maybe it's more than that. Twenty-odd years is a lot of work for a family reunion."

"Now you're thinking," he approved. "I've met David. Tell me about your sisters."

I told him about Lia and Aria, the Moon and Judgement. I told him about how I'd tracked Paul Sheffield for a while, but then how thrilled Dad had been when the Card shifted to Aria like he'd always hoped it would. I told him about how we'd tracked them, followed them, and ultimately kidnapped them. To his credit, Rhys didn't throw me out of the van as we were driving at 45 miles per hour. Finally, I told him about how things had been going with David, and how Dad had reached the end of his rope with the kid and locked him in his room.

"I don't think David's going to respond real well to that," Rhys observed. "He hates being controlled as much as I do, from what I can tell. Plus, he seems to have more of an angry rebellious streak. I imagine that being contrary is in the blood of Devils."

"I know. This is turning ugly, just like it did with Lia and Aria."

Rhys steered the van into a gas station, but parked along the edge rather than at the pump. Then he turned stern eyes to me. I didn't even know he could look stern.

"I'm not going to sugar-coat it, Zora. You've been up to some pretty nasty karmic stuff, and even if your dad sort of brainwashed you, you own a good bit of it yourself."

"Tell me something I don't know," I pouted.

"Alright, I will. I think this is why the Pattern brought me to you right now. You had to see the truth before it was too late. Destiny doesn't work like the romantics of the world think it does. There's a Pattern of key events, but humans' free will determines the ultimate design. Your decisions here are everything now that your eyes are open."

"What am I supposed to do?"

He shrugged and his blue eyes began to shift from the hue of a sunny summer sky to the slate of a stormy day. His voice became more resonant, as if he were standing in an enormous, empty room. Maybe I couldn't see his chakras, but I knew this was the Fool's power at work. "Even if I knew, I couldn't tell you. This is *your* moment to influence the Pattern. So far, the fallout has been minimal, but it won't stay that way. Everything has been building toward *now*. No matter what you choose to do, the consequences will be life-altering. This is a time of great convergence, and once you choose your course, the dominoes will begin to fall."

"The alignment!" I realized. "This all comes back to the planetary alignment!"

"Planetary alignments mark pivotal endings and new beginnings, particularly to us with magical blood." The echo in his voice was a little unnerving, but it also felt like I was getting advice from a higher place, not just a person. "We are approaching a major energy shift and a time of transformation, and you are more a part of that than you have ever been. You are coming of age, spiritually speaking, Zora, and your choices will have ripples that affect many, not just yourself. Reach within and decide who you are." He finished his sentence, and the summer sky returned to his eyes. He shivered violently like when you get an unexpected chill out of nowhere. "Whoa ... that was intense!" He grinned at me. "That hasn't happened in a while!"

"Was that ... was that your deity speaking through you or something?"

"Sort of, I guess. I don't really have a deity like other Arcana do. I commune with my Higher Self, which is tapped into the truths of the Universe. It's wicked Transcendental! But," he continued, his face growing serious for a moment, "it was also really important, what I said. You can't just deflect responsibility this time. You have to decide how to go forward with *intention*."

My mind pushed back, grieving the loss of whatever childlike mindset I might have left. "What if I just don't do anything? Just walk away or stand back, or whatever? Just not help Dad anymore?"

"It's like Rush sang back in the day: *If you choose not to decide, you still have made a choice.*"

"That's deep."

"It's my mom's favorite song. One of mine, too, I guess. Kind of the Fool's Anthem."

My phone vibrated with an incoming text from Dad.

Come home immediately.

I didn't even have to ask what had happened, because I knew: David just realized he'd been caged and was going bonkers. No doubt Dad was hoping I could talk the kid down. But the question was: would I? Or would I choose to defy my father for the first time in my life and just let David out of his suburban prison?

"I've got to go home," I told Rhys. "Can you drop me a few houses down?"

"Yeah, of course. I can get gas later. Is everything okay?"

"David's probably just hit the roof because he's realized he's trapped. Dad's no good at handling him."

"What are you going to do?"

"I don't know exactly, but I don't think my dad is going to like it." I pulled up the photo I'd taken earlier and stared at the last peaceful image I'd probably ever have of Dad. I knew in my heart I was about to blow everything up.

"Is that him?" Rhys asked. I nodded and turned the phone to show him. Rhys grew pale, then reached across me to the glove box. He whipped it open and a stack of papers, wet wipes, pens and other gubbins dumped everywhere. He was literally laying across my lap as he rooted around, searching for something. After a moment, he found his prize and handed it to me: a rusty-hued vintage Polaroid of a shirtless, dark-haired man lounging on a striped blanket and holding a beer. The man in the photo smiled rakishly at the camera, or at whoever was holding it. The picture had *D. in Sedona, 2000* scrawled across the bottom.

My breath caught in my throat as I stared at the pictures side-by-side. Even with the years in between the images, the similarities were undeniable.

D. in Sedona stood for Dorian. My father. Rhys's father.

Rhys was my brother. And Dad didn't know about him.

Chapter 11

We rode in silence for a few minutes, staring straight ahead. Rhys finally spoke. I texted Dad to tell him I was on my way, but he didn't respond. I was grateful for that.

"Well, I guess that's why the Pattern so strongly pushed me in your direction."

"Ya think?" I didn't mean to sound so sour, but my mind was reeling. This was a lot of change to take in within a very short time span.

"Yeah, I think. Should I … you know … come in and introduce myself? It kinda feels like I shouldn't."

"Given everything that's been going on lately, I'm going with a hard NO on that. If Dad doesn't know about you, that's a good thing."

"This is messed up," was all he could think to say. I imagined it was pretty hard to strike Rhys speechless.

"Truer words were never spoken." I took a deep breath. "Listen, I have to get David out of there, and I think you're the ace up my sleeve. I'll text you tonight, but I think I need to get the kid to calm down and slip him out tonight. Then you can take him somewhere."

Rhys nodded. "Maybe I can take him to Mom for a little while. He might even like it there since she's so chill."

"Good idea. Even if he doesn't want to stay there, at least he'll be away from all of this. I don't know how they're going to feel about it, but I'll reach out to Lia and Aria. They should know what's going on."

"Did you say Lia was in Florida?"

"Yeah, St. Augustine."

"That's about an hour and a half, two hours from Cassadaga." The wheels in his mind were turning, and I had to give him credit. Other than knowing I needed to get David out of town, my brain was a bowl of oatmeal. Should I leave with David? Or should I stay and try to make sure Dad couldn't do whatever ritual he was cooking up? It was all too much to think about, but I had no choice.

Rhys turned onto the street parallel to the house and drove to the end of the block. "I'm going to drop you here so that I don't have to drive by the house. I can pick David up in the same spot."

"I'll text you," I nodded. "I don't know how much of a row they've gotten into, but it's going to take my last brain cell to settle everything down and send them both to their respective corners without looking sketchy. I don't know how long it will be before you hear from me, but I'll send you something before dark."

"That works. I'll call Mom and give her a heads-up." He rolled to a stop at the far end of the street.

"Thanks. As messed up as this is, and it's a right disaster, I'm glad you're here. It's nice to have a sibling I didn't kidnap." He smirked and I jumped out, slamming the door behind me.

I ran up the street toward the house. It'd been almost 15 minutes since my Dad's text, which wasn't too bad if he thought I was out walking the neighborhood. I jogged up to the front door, bracing myself for who-knew-what inside. But when I stepped inside, all I heard was the whimpering of one of the dogs.

"Dad? David?" I called. I walked through the foyer into the great room. Dad was sitting on the ottoman, facing the picture window that looked out onto the woods. It was Tess who was upstairs crying. "Dad? What's going on?"

He stood and turned to me, and I recoiled. I'd never seen him like this, not even when Mum died. His eyes were red and swollen, and he stared at me like he'd never seen me before.

"I didn't think ..." he began, but then lost his words.

"Dad, what's happened?"

"He was so *angry* ..."

I turned and looked up the stairway, and saw that the brace hadn't been removed from David's door. "David, I'm going to get you out of there!" He didn't answer, but I heard Dad muttering something behind me. I ran up the stairs and bustled the dog out of the way, and she started barking and hopping around behind me. I grabbed the release bar from the next room and, after struggling with it for a moment, whipped the apparatus off the doorframe and pulled the bedroom door open.

Tess ran in ahead of me. The room was empty and the window was wide open, the screen lying bent on the far side of the bed. This wasn't good. Because of the walk-out basement, David's room was nearly three stories above the ground. Tess had her paws up on the sill, looking outward. I ran to the window and looked down. There was no way he would have jumped from here. Even David wasn't that crazy.

I turned back to question Dad, and found him standing at the bedroom door, still clearly in shock. "Maybe he thought he could get a good grip on the stones and make his way to the upstairs patio ..."

I had an awful feeling in the pit of my stomach, and slowly turned back toward the window and stuck my head out. I placed my hand on the exterior stones and peered toward the balcony. The stones were solid with deep grooves of mortar between them. It might be do-able for an experienced rock climber. Which David wasn't, as far as I knew.

My heart was in my throat as I dropped my gaze along the edge of the house to the basement patio below. I knew what I would see. I didn't want to look, but I had to.

It was a sight I'd never be able to erase from my memory.

David's limp body lay sprawled face-up next to the fire pit, a dark stain running from beneath his head out into the edge of the grass. A river rock from the edge of the pit had been dislodged when he fell. When his head hit it.

I leaned out the window and retched up the tea I'd drunk earlier.

I'd gained one brother and lost another in the same day.

The damn dog was barking incessantly, but I could barely even hear it.

Some minutes later I found my dad sitting where he'd been when I arrived home.

"Did you call 911?" It was the only thing I found the words to ask him.

He hung his head. "It was too late. He was yelling, swearing he'd escape and then we'd be sorry. I tried to reason with him, tried to explain, but he wasn't having it ..." He buried his face in his hands. "I heard him rummaging around, but I assumed he was looking for his phone. I never thought ..." His voice broke. It was nearly a minute before he managed to continue. "I sat down at the table here, and even over Tess' barking, I heard him banging about above my head. I didn't hear the window open. I swear I would have run upstairs if I'd heard it ... and then I saw him fall ..." He looked at me then, his eyes almost pleading.

"Dad, what are we going to do? We have to call the police or an ambulance or something." I tried to sound reasonable, but sobs were wracking my entire body. *David, I'm sorry* ... I couldn't help feeling like I could have reasoned with him if only I hadn't gone out.

"We can't, Zora. Don't you see? He wasn't here legally. If the police got involved, they'd figure out who he was eventually, and there may even be video of you two together somewhere. You're not a minor, Zora. You'd run the risk of ..."

"Of what? Kidnapping charges?" The words flew out before I was able to stop them. I did, however, manage to choke back the venomous spew of accusations that were about to follow. "We can't just leave him there!"

"No, no, of course not." My flash of anger seemed to push my father into action. "This was a horrible accident, Zora. But it was just that: an accident. We'll wrap him up and wait till dark. Then we'll go bury him properly. We can't call the authorities, but we can still honor him."

Was this man completely delusional? Once he'd shaken off his initial shock and grief, he had immediately switched over to damage control. I stared at him, seeing him clearly for perhaps the first time. Everything was a calculation. Even his own children. Maybe especially his own children.

"You're right, Zora. We can't leave him there. We have to move him immediately." He went into the pantry and emerged with a box of trash bags, then rummaged around in a kitchen drawer until he found the roll of packing tape.

My jaw nearly hit the floor. What was this? An episode of a crime drama? "Zora, my girl, I know this is horrible, and we'll have time to grieve, but we must take action. I can't do this without you."

How many times had he said some version of those words to me over the past year? I felt his powers of persuasion pressing against me, something I wouldn't have noticed a week ago.

Still, he was right about one thing: any ties to David would be traced directly to me. I thought about the rent-a-cops in North Carolina who hadn't reported us, but might have put a warning in some system or other. I knew that the whole situation had been arranged to keep Dad's hands clean, something he'd learned from our experiences with Lia and Aria.

He placed his hand on my arm, and I fought the urge to cringe. "Dearest, we must take care of the task at hand."

He led me downstairs to the basement, and I could see David's legs splayed out from behind the firepit. I think a small part of me was hoping it was some elaborate illusion magic, staged to make us suffer for trapping him.

If only.

Tess followed us down and took up a position weeping by the glass door when we shut her inside.

Dad lifted David's head and shoulders so I wouldn't have to look my brother in his glazed eyes, but I couldn't help myself. The back of his mousy hair was matted with blood and his neck bent in an unnatural angle. I maneuvered his legs and feet, fighting the urge to scream, vomit, and cry all at once. Together, we wrapped him in plastic and taped it up tight, then Dad got the hose and rinsed the blood off the flagstones while I sat on the ground and wept.

I didn't tell Dad that I'd spotted the Devil card in David's sock.

Let the Card be buried with him. It was a small gesture, but it was the only act of rebellion I could think to commit for my unfailingly-rebellious brother.

Chapter 12

Dad and I barely spoke for the rest of the day. He shut himself up in his room for about an hour, then took off in his car without a word to me. He was gone for a couple of hours, then came back in and returned to his side of the house. I just sat in the great room and stared out the window at the trees in the backyard. I watched as the sun moved across the treetops and the shadows lengthened. I cried a few times, but the tears were eventually replaced by a hollowness that completely enveloped me.

Around 6:00, I pulled out my phone, set it to silent, and sent a message to Rhys:

David tried 2 escape when he woke up and fell from the 2nd floor. He's dead.

After a few seconds, a reply came in.

OMG. What do you need me to do?

I can't think straight. Dad says we're going 2 bury him after dark. I have no idea what 2 do.

Are you safe?

I think so.

I'll stay in the church lot. I can be to you in 3 min if you need me.

Thx. And then, as an afterthought, I sent, **Don't follow us 2nite. I don't want him 2 sense u.**

Rhys sent back the thumbs-up emoji.

When the dark finally came, Dad emerged from his suite and ushered me into the garage. He pulled his SUV out and backed it up as far as the edge of the house, then handed me a pair of work gloves. He put on a pair as well, and motioned for me to follow him. We walked along the treed property line until we reached the basement patio, where our grim package still lay wrapped and nestled against the wall.

Dad went to lift David's top half, but I stopped him. Something in me didn't want Dad to ever touch David again.

"No."

He stood back up and opened his mouth to protest, but I didn't give him the chance.

"This is my job," I insisted, but what I was really thinking was, *He was my responsibility.*

I reached out to Shakti, something I'd been afraid to do all day. I felt her presence, full of sadness. The sadness was a comfort; I had expected the rage of Kali, goddess of destruction and death, to be waiting for me. I had read about her when I was younger, and of all Shakti's faces, Kali's was the only one I feared.

Shakti filled me with power, and I reached down and lifted David as though he weighed next to nothing. I carried him, wrapped in his plastic shroud, as though he were a sleeping child being carried to bed. My heart chakra filled my entire body with jagged pain, and when I laid my brother in the open back of the SUV, the strength flowed away and left me depleted and empty. My shoulders and upper back felt leaden.

I pushed the button to close the boot and walked around the front of the car. I got in the passenger side without even looking at my father, even when he got in and started the engine.

He shifted into gear and started to pull out, but stopped before reaching the end of the driveway.

"Things are bleak, Zora, but we need each other now. We've always had each other to lean on, and that hasn't changed."

Was that supposed to be comforting? I nodded, but couldn't even bring myself to turn my head in his direction.

"We'll be okay, my girl, you'll see." He touched my forearm, and it was all I could do not to recoil from the gesture.

He started driving, and as we drove past the church, I noted the dark van out of the corner of my eye. I was so glad Dad didn't know about Rhys. At least one brother would stay safe, untouched. Uncorrupted.

I lost track of where we were going, but after about 45 minutes, Dad pulled onto a road that ran alongside a construction site. He was careful to stay on the pavement.

"They poured the concrete for those footings today, and it will still be plenty wet." He pointed at several points along the edge of the new construction, each about the size of a large bathtub.

"So you want me to just chuck him in there, do you?"

"Zora, this is what must be done to protect you ... to protect us both. I wish it didn't have to be this way."

Venomous thoughts filled my mind as I got out of the car and popped the hatch. Tapping into my power again, I lifted David and carried him across the dark construction site to one of the footings in the center. I found one that had settled somewhat and wasn't filled all the way to the top and lowered David's body into the wet cement. I watched him sink below the surface, and I knew I should immediately head back to the car, but somehow that felt *wrong*. Not that any of this was right.

I had failed him in life; I didn't want to fail him in death. What if plunking him in this building foundation cursed him to haunt the building? I didn't want to doom his soul to that. Nor did I want his angry spirit to bring suffering to innocent people who might live or work here someday.

Shakti, I prayed, *help me figure out how to put his soul to rest.*

His is a troubled soul, not yet destined for eternal freedom and peace.

Is he going to be a ghost?

He may choose that route. At least until his soul is born again to continue its evolution.

She was talking about reincarnation. Too heavy a subject for me to get into with her right now.

How can I give his soul peace?

That is not within my scope, Zora. But you may give him a final prayer. If his soul is near, he may hear you.

Not exactly the advice I'd been hoping for, but it was all I was likely to get.

"David," I whispered. "David, I'm so sorry. If I'd known ..." I broke off what I was saying. He didn't need my excuses. "I wish I'd handled all this differently. I ... I don't know if you can hear me, but if you can, don't stay in this place with your body. Come with me. Stay with me. If that means you haunt me forever, then okay. At least you won't be stuck here, and you won't be alone. And maybe I can find a way for you to be at peace. You deserved better than this, kid. I—" My voice fell away, knowing no words would ever be enough. "I'll find a way to stop him, David. I swear it."

I couldn't think of anything else to say, so I scuffed away my footprints as best I could as I made my way back to where Dad was waiting.

***

We each retreated to our respective rooms when we returned home, and I shot Rhys a text telling him I was okay and that I'd talk to him the next day. I lay in bed, numb, staring at the ceiling fan as it spun round. I'm not sure when I fell asleep, but I awoke to the gray light of dawn peeking through my blinds.

I also had a splitting headache, no doubt because of all the crying I'd done the day before. I downed a couple of pain tabs and headed downstairs for a cup of tea. I poured a little cream in the bottom of my cup as I waited for the electric kettle to heat up. If ever a day called for strong black English Breakfast tea, this was that day. The hot water had just clicked to READY when Dad shuffled in. I couldn't bring myself to look at him. Darcy padded along beside him, and Dad filled the dogs' bowls with food. Darcy had the food to himself, as Tess had resumed her vigil by David's bedroom door.

I couldn't help blaming him even more than I blamed myself for David's death. But I also didn't know what to do about it. I felt paralyzed from the neck up.

He went to the coffee machine and plugged in a capsule, letting the automation of the device do the rest. I could feel his eyes boring into the side of my head.

"Zora, my girl, we must talk. Yesterday was an unspeakable tragedy, and you've been so tough ... but there's more to be done. I wish we could spend a month grieving the boy, but we can't. The alignment is less than a week away, and if we don't figure out how to harness some of your sisters' energy, all of this—all of it—will have been for naught."

"How can you even think about that right now?" I muttered, though the words in my head were much less polite.

"It's only because I must. I didn't sleep a wink. I was researching arcane theory all night long trying to figure out how to make the ritual work without having to have Lia and Aria present."

I couldn't believe what I was hearing. His son died less than a day ago, and he was still trying to calculate all the angles. I stared at the kettle, pondering what to say. "Why is it so important to you to unite the Arcana? You've always said we could save the world from itself if we were all united, but this seems more ... personal." I didn't want to challenge him directly, especially now that I was starting to think he was actually completely mad. But I had to know what could possibly be worth all the effort he'd gone to.

And what could be so important that he could brush David's death aside so easily?

My father had never been prone to outbursts of emotionality; in fact, he's never been prone to showing much emotion at all. But at this moment, he took my hands in his and turned me to face him.

"Zora, you're right that this is much bigger than an altruistic motive to make the world a less chaotic place. There's a great deal of family history involved, and wrongs that must be righted. I'm not sure I can even take the time to explain it all to you in a way that will make sense."

"So tell me what you have time for, then." I tried to keep the acid out of my voice, and I could feel my solar plexus chakra pulsating, calling me to embrace my personal power. I allowed the power to flow through me like molten gold, filling me with resolve to do whatever needed to be done to thwart Dad's plans and keep the rest of my siblings safe.

"I need to meet with a real estate agent in a little over an hour, but hold on ... I have a book of family history which will get you started, and then I can answer any questions you have when I get back."

"When will that be?" I filled a tea strainer with loose tea leaves and poured the steaming water on top of the cream. It was everything I could do to pretend that I wasn't brimming with rage.

"I have several different sites to survey." He offered no explanation for why he was out shopping for real estate, even though I raised an eyebrow in his direction. "I will be back mid-afternoon, I expect. But I'll bring the book to the small office upstairs. You'll need to wear gloves when you handle it."

That caught me by surprise. Dad didn't usually get out the books that were old enough to require the gloves. I had tried looking at them when I was younger, but when I nearly spilled soda on one, he put most of them away. Only a couple, like the one he'd let Aria see, were in the main part of the house. He kept them in his private study in the owners suite. When we first moved here, it was a second walk-in closet, and he had had it modified to control humidity and dust.

"Are you sure you want to leave one of those out here with me?" I admit it, I was feeling petty. The jab wasn't lost on him.

"I'm sure I can trust you not to bring food or drink near it, my dear. Please just keep the blinds in that room closed so it doesn't get any direct sunlight, and I'll return it to my study when I get home. It's long past the time you should have learned all of this, I suppose."

"So why haven't I heard about it before now? Some deep, dark secrets lurking in the family archives?"

"Not exactly, but much of what we can glean from our early history came in journals, so without historical context ..."

"That doesn't really answer the question."

"No, I suppose not. Let me just say this: the journal I'm going to let you peruse is perhaps our most sacred family possession. It dates back to the 16th century, you see. Back to the days when the Arcana were one united body. To the best of my knowledge, it is the only volume in existence chronicling the decision to split the Cards up." His voice took on an angry edge. "Our forebears were charged with a sacred task in keeping these records, at great cost to ourselves."

He fell silent and I stared at him for an uncomfortable moment. Then he seemed to shake off the mood that had grasped him and sipped his coffee. The anger in his eyes disappeared as quickly as it had emerged.

I wasn't quite sure what to say, and felt like I needed to tread carefully. "Sounds like it contains some important information."

"Yes, yes indeed," he nodded emphatically. "I wasn't intentionally keeping information from you, it just never seemed the right time to delve into it all. It's a story of politics, revolution, and betrayal."

The 16th century? Something tickled the back of my mind. "Is this connected to why we never went to any of the Guy Fawkes festivities?"

The anger flashed in his eyes again, and he nodded, his jaw set.

"Maybe that would have been a good time to tell me about it, so I wouldn't have been salty about missing the fireworks." I regretted my snark as soon as the words left my mouth. I was playing a dangerous game with an unstable man.

He waited a moment before responding, perhaps trying to tamp down rage of his own. "You were too young to understand then. Now you're not." He set his coffee down and strode into his suite, returning a few moments later with a book meticulously wrapped in a 4-flap covering of blinding white acid-free paper. He carried it up the stairs into the room with the writing desk, and I heard the tell-tale sound of mini-blinds being twisted shut.

His footsteps were heavy as he stomped back down the stairs. "I've left it on the desk, and you know the gloves are there in the drawer. Remember to wrap the book if you're going to step away, even for a few minutes. I'll see you after my appointment with the realtor."

Without even a passing glance in my direction, he snagged his coffee and retreated to his rooms to get ready.

I had some getting ready to do, too. But this time, the agenda was my own. I pulled out my phone and scrolled to Aria's cell number.

Hey, sis. The game has changed, and so have I. We need to talk. -Z.

Chapter 13

I'm not an idiot. Of course I took pictures of every single page of the journal. Then I texted them all to Rhys. I was just happy that they were in English and not Latin. Shakespeare's English at the beginning, I'll grant you. They were even mostly legible and shockingly not written in some sort of code or cipher, which I'd been half-expecting.

Rhys wanted to pick me up right away, to get me out of the house ... away from our father, and away from danger. But I knew I had to play a longer game. It was entirely possible that I could get away and disappear, especially with Rhys's help. But Dad also knew where Aria and Lia were, and it was my job now to keep them safe, too. The only way I could do that was to flip the script.

It took Aria a while to get back to me, and I couldn't blame her. I'm sure she rallied her cousins and aunt, and was preparing for war if it came to that. But we hadn't parted on the worst of terms, so I had hope.

Lia was another story altogether. There was no way she'd respond to any message from me. That's why I had to get Aria on board first, and it wasn't going to be easy. She made that clear in her response text.

I don't want anything to do with you.

I get it. But I need 2 talk 2u. Important things r happening here and they involve u whether u want them 2 or not.

There was a pause before she texted back.

I'm not helping you or him.

Just hear me out. No secrets. U can have ur family on speaker. I need ur help.

I planned every word, expecting that somehow my father would see them.

Fine. Call me.

Thank u. Give me 15 mins.

K.

Good sign. If I could get her to talk to me, I was pretty sure I could make her understand. But I couldn't do it alone. I needed Rhys. I texted him and told him to meet me down the road. I didn't want any of the outdoor cameras to pick him up stopping in front of the house. Once I was safely in his van, I breathed a sigh of relief.

He looped around and pulled into the church parking lot, and didn't say a word the whole time. Once he cut the engine, though, he turned and looked at me for a moment, then grabbed me into a bear hug and held me tight.

"I'm so glad you're safe." His voice cracked a little, and the emotion caught me by surprise. I realized at that moment that he was the first person who'd truly been looking out for me since my mother died. The thought broke me, and I melted against him, sobbing. "It's okay now," he assured me. "I've got you. We'll get through this."

Hugging wasn't really something I was used to, so I didn't make it more than about 30 seconds before pulling back, sniffling. I wiped my eyes with the back of my thumb. "Thanks, mate."

"Not mate," he corrected me. "I'm your brother. Your big brother. A week ago, I didn't know I had any family except for my mom. Now I've got a whole litter of you. I've already lost one, and I'm not losing any more."

I felt a buzzing in my heart chakra, and it grew outward, electrifying each of the other ones as the power spread. I felt like I was lit up like a rainbow Christmas tree. I could feel myself pulsating in perfect alignment.

"Whoa." Rhys leaned back, studying my aura.

"Wait, you can see auras now?"

"Not usually, no. But I can see the Pattern at key moments in time, and ..."

"What does that mean, see the Pattern?"

"Well, like, we all have free will, like I said, but there are important events in the Universe's Pattern that are fixed. We can choose how we respond to them, but the moments are like intersections in an enormous map. When I'm near one of those moments, I can see those different paths like tendrils of white light. Right now, a bunch of them are converging on you. You're like a 10-way stop light right now."

"Is that good or bad?"

"Could be either one. But it tells me that you've made a very important choice, one that's going to have a pretty big ripple effect on the Pattern."

I still wasn't sure I understood, but it felt like what he was saying affirmed what I was planning to do. "I did make a decision. We have to stop Dad, whatever it takes. You, me, Aria, Lia ... all of us. We have to work together to make sure his plan fails."

"What is his plan? Is it in all those pages you sent me pictures of?"

"I think the motive came from there, but before we try to read all of those, we have to rally the troops." I pulled out my phone. Aria would be waiting for my call by this point.

"So we're going to call one of our sisters?"

I nodded. "We're going to call Aria. She doesn't totally hate me, I don't think, but she doesn't trust me either. If I can get her on board, I'm hoping she can get Lia."

I hit the dial button on Aria's number and took a deep breath. The power around me was down to a soft hum, but I could still feel it dancing up and down the center of my body like seven pinwheels spinning at different speeds.

"Hello, Zora." Aria's voice was tinged with the edge of anger. I guess I couldn't really expect it to be otherwise ... I had been complicit in a scheme that hurt one of her cousins and her aunt, and forcibly brought her here to Atlanta. I really had to ask her one of these days how she'd managed to get back home.

"Hey, sis."

"I don't think I like you calling me that."

"Duly noted. And you're right. But we have a bigger problem, and ..."

"Somehow, your problems don't feel like they need to be my problems." Yeah, she was still pretty salty.

"Is anyone there with you? Am I on speaker?"

She paused, but then answered, "Yes. Logan and Paul are here."

"Good. They should probably know about this, too." I heard a rustling around on her end, and I could picture them exchanging dubious glances. "I have someone here with me, too. Someone you should meet."

"Oh, Lord. Another one? Another Arcana spawn?"

Rhys sputtered with laughter. "Oh, I like her." He leaned in toward the mic. "Hey, Aria. I'm your older brother Rhys."

"And before you say anything else, *sis*," I emphasized, hoping she would understand it was a blood-tie thing and not an I'm-trying-to-annoy-you thing, "you should know that I did *not* kidnap him. He found me. And Dad doesn't know about him."

"Say what now? How could he not know?"

"Well, that's a little bit of an odd story, but suffice to say that I'm the product of a music festival hook-up ..."

"What are the freaking odds ..." Disbelief rather than rage. I considered that progress.

"Yeah, I guess he has a type, even if he didn't know it at the time. I've been thinking about it, and maybe being around my mom's energy is what made him think of this whole insane baby-making plan."

It astonished me how Rhys was able to pull Aria into comfortable conversation so easily. It was definitely one of his superpowers. I wished I could let him handle the entire negotiation, but that task was mine alone. "Aria, listen, I know that I'm one of the last people you want to talk to. Like you probably hoped to forget this arm of your family even existed. But we have to stop whatever Dad has planned for the planetary alignment. You know he wanted to reunite the Arcana, but the more I think about it, the more I think he wants to siphon some of our power for God-knows-what. We can't let him."

"Well, if I'm two states away, he can't very well siphon mine."

"I'm not sure that's true. He's been doing a lot of research about how to tap into not only your powers, but Lia's, too. I think we need to take the fight to him—proactively."

"Forgive me for being the doubting Thomas," came a voice I recognized as Paul's. I hadn't heard it since he had been Judgement. Back then, I'd called him a few times to try and get a bead on him, even though he wasn't one of Dad's offspring. "You've been your father's little errand girl for years, why the sudden change of heart? Why should we trust you?"

I'd been prepared for this question, but my emotions were still raw when I answered. "Because we had another brother—David, the kid I went to New York to pick up—and now he's dead." I heard gasps from the other end of the line. "We didn't kill him; he died in an accident. But he never even should have been here. He should be ... should be ..." I couldn't get the words out. *He should be alive and well in New York. Not dead and buried in the concrete foundation of a building in Georgia.*

"What Zora's trying to tell you," Rhys broke in, "is that her eyes are open now. Her father—*our* father—has been subtly gaslighting and controlling her for years, and it's only recently she's started to realize it. She understands that whatever his purpose is, it can't be good. And we owe it to David to stop him."

Rhys and I spent the next twenty minutes explaining to Aria what had happened since she'd left. As the embodiment of Judgement, she was deeply distressed about what had transpired with David, and that there was no one to answer for it.

"I'm going to make him pay, Zora. You should know that. If he's not going to answer to the law, he's going to answer to me. And because of the way Judgement works, you might be answering to me, too."

"I accept that," I answered her, and in a weird way, I felt a little bit relieved that there might be some sort of reckoning coming for me. Paying some sort of price might be the only way for me to feel absolved.

"We have to talk to my mom about this," Logan began, and there was no doubt he felt I needed to pay some sort of price for my role in this whole ridiculous master plan of Dad's, "but I think she'll want him stopped. We'll be flying in, most likely. When's the alignment?"

"In four days." I could feel the knot in my chest loosening. They didn't have to like me to agree with me, and I was grateful that they understood that.

"Look, we aren't letting Aria come alone. The only question is whether there will be three of us or four of us coming. Do you have a problem with that?"

"No. And even if I did, it's your right to do what you think is best. But you also need to understand that there may be parts of it that Aria has to do without you. You don't have Arcana powers, and short of extreme violence, that's the only thing that can stop my father."

"The last thing we want is for anyone on our side to get hurt," Rhys assured the Sheffield cousins. "Having some extra muscle around can't be a bad thing, but Zora's right. We'd like to avoid violence if we can, but we'd also like to avoid any of us having to suffer the consequences of violence, mental or physical."

"Somehow, I don't think I'd suffer too greatly if I got to jack Blair right in the jaw." Logan was the athlete of the family, and could do some serious physical damage on a normal person if the situation arose. But this wasn't that kind of situation, and it was far more likely that my father would be able to use his Arcana abilities to convince Logan to hurt himself. It wouldn't be the first time, and despite his bravado, Logan knew that.

"We'll deal with that as it comes," I jumped in before the revenge fantasies started taking us off course. "But Aria, will you call Lia? I know you've never met her, but …"

"I'll convince her," Aria snapped, "don't worry." She took Lia's and Rhys's numbers and then we signed off.

"I don't like the idea of you going back to that house."

"I'll be okay, Rhys. If he knows I've convinced Aria to come, he'll be too happy to doubt my loyalty. And I need to get back so that I can read some of that journal before he gets home."

"Alright, but I want a text from you every hour so that I know you're okay. I'm going to be on stakeout over here."

I smiled at him, feeling profoundly grateful for his being there. "I agree to your terms on the condition that you go to one of the highway truck stops and take a damn shower."

He grinned wide. "That bad?"

"That bad."

Chapter 14

I'd been struggling to decipher late 16th century spelling for nearly an hour, and my eyes were going wonky. I leaned back in the antique chair and stretched my back, and the old wood groaned in protest under the strain. Then I slipped off the gloves and got up and walked across the room to where my water bottle sat on a small side table in the corner, far away from Dad's precious manuscript.

Darcy and Tess spotted my movement from the family room below and trotted to the bottom of the stairs, chuffing at me in hopes of food or a walk. I had to get as much reading in as I could before Dad got home, so the pups would have to settle for a handful of biscuits for the mo.

Once that was sorted, I slipped the gloves back on for another round. The manuscript wasn't easy to read, but I had learned some things I didn't expect. Arcana families, at least in my experience, tended to be rather flexible in the spirituality department. While I had only met a handful, not a one of them had been a devotee of any particular faith. I chalked that up to the understanding that came with the inheritance of a Card: that all divine energies were representation of some aspect of the Universe, and that there wasn't any real paradox with all these energies existing, because they were manifestations of how humans understood the Universal Spirit.

What surprised me in the journal was that the first entries I came across, those of Sir William Catesby of Warwickshire, indicated that my ancestors, at least in that time period, were devout Catholics. Sir William's divine energy was that of the Catholic God. He used his abilities of persuasion to bolster the faith of other Catholics around him, as it was a faith under a good deal of persecution at that time in England, particularly after King Henry VIII's formation of the Church of England in 1534.

Most of Sir William's journals were testaments to his faith:

I taketh joy and comfort in the fact that I have endeavored to preach the truth plainly and glorify my blessed Lord. I am sad, though, in seeing that so few are willing to risk bodily harm in defense of the One True Faith. I seek to turn hearts toward our faith, yet I cannot blame people for being afear'd of consequence. It is all I can do to provide a private place where they may worship Our Lord in peace, away from prying eyes. The state of things is less encouraging than it was one year ago. My heart hath known what it is to be imprisoned for loving Our Lord, and not all people have the strength of heart to suffer so.

I found it odd that there was no mention of the Cards at all. Only of Sir William's *blessed gift in touching hearts and stirring courage with words.* Sir William's handwriting ended in 1598, and that's when I decided to give my eyes a break. I looked at my watch: 11:24. I should have at least a couple of hours before Dad returned home, and I could only hope that the reading would get easier as the language and spelling got closer to something I could understand more easily.

I walked around the house for a couple of minutes to restore circulation in my bum, then headed back to the dim room and the creaky chair. I slipped the gloves back on and turned the page to read the next entry.

It is with a heavy heart that I take this book in my hands for the first time, having received it from my mother only days ago. My father is one with Christ, and so I cannot weep for him. But I weep for those of us who will miss him deeply. As he passed to God's Kingdom, I felt as though the earthly strength he will no longer need passed to me. What a worthy inheritance, to stand as strongly with God as my father before me. May I be some portion of the man he was.

And then it was signed: *Robert Catesby, 1598.*

Something in the back of my brain started rattling. Catesby ... I knew that name somehow, though I didn't recall my father ever speaking of our ancestors, at least not by name.

Robert Catesby ... Robert Catesby ...

I slipped the gloves off and pulled out my phone. I sent Rhys a thumbs-up emoji, then searched for the name.

The search results nearly made me drop my phone in shock.

"ROBERT CATESBY (c. 1572–8 November 1605) was the leader of a group of English Catholics who planned the failed Gunpowder Plot of 1605 ..."

My jaw hung open ... I was distantly descended from the man responsible for the plot to blow up Parliament in 1605? Somehow that made a stupid amount of sense, given my father's temperament. I had learned about the Gunpowder Plot when we studied the reason for the November 5th Bonfire Night back at primary school, in the same way that American school children probably learn about Billy the Kid and the Wild West. Guy Fawkes got all the press, but Catesby had been the mastermind.

I couldn't wait to tell Rhys about this. I'm sure he'd be reading the pages, too, but given that his education was as unconventional as mine, I doubted he'd understand the significance.

I didn't find direct references to his infamous activities in 1605, which was a little disappointing, if I'm honest. In fact, Robert Catesby himself didn't write in the journal all that often, but when he did, his entries were prayers or angry and even violent rants against the Crown's treatment of Catholics. There was, however, one notable exception.

15th June, 1604

I hesitate to put these words to paper, but a record of this must be kept. My father told me in my youth that we numbered twenty-two families who had inherited from our Creator the power to influence the world away from wickedness. Each of the families had unique and wondrous abilities with which they had been blessed for this purpose.

Religious intolerance is a scourge in these times. Catholics are pressed if they will not turn their hearts from the One True Faith, and hanged in the public square if they do. Jews are burned alive in Spain, I hear, and certainly those of uncertain faith have suffered to be burned as witches in many countries.

I received correspondence today that one of these families, who I will not name on these pages in case the book should fall to evil hands, has called for a conference of all of us in four months' time. There is great fear among our number, the letter said, because of those very blessings, and the writer has devised a plan to protect that which we have been given, so that it may survive these dark times and light the world in future generations.

May God be with us.

I found myself staring at the yellowed page and archaic words, and couldn't believe what I was seeing. Catesby was talking about the Arcana! No wonder William's entries hadn't mentioned the Cards ... they hadn't been created at that time!

My eyes devoured the next few pages, looking for more. I found it in an entry dated only a year and a handful of days prior to the events that would lead to Catesby's death.

2nd November, 1604

The deed has been done. The man who wrote the letter I received some months ago brought the twenty-two of us together in an abandoned abbey in Sussex, and I am unsure how I feel about what transpired. I felt that the Lord was with me, yet the conclave itself was filled with non-believers. I did recognize a half-dozen familiar English faces in the group, though I was not acquainted with them personally.

When our host brought out a card game he brought with him from Italy, I feared that I had been duped, and expected agents of the Scot king to crash in on us at any moment. I was assured by others in the group that even if there were a passerby among the hills, they would proceed without noticing us. They were certain of this, they told me, as misdirection of the mind was among their gifts. I was not reassured.

Nevertheless, we kept company undisturbed for an hour as the moon rose high into the sky. The Italian gentleman was an astronomer of sorts, he claimed, and said that the sky favored our intention on that evening alone. At any rate, it was this fellow's intention to create a partial deck of cards similar to the ones he had brought with him, utilizing specially treated parchment.

Each of us chose one of the cards in the deck and placed it beside a piece of parchment of similar size, then placed a drop of our own blood on the parchment to seal our oath to our descendents. The Italian offered his prayers and the drops of blood became as ink on the blank paper, recreating the cards that we had selected. Then we were to take these newly created cards with us as we parted ways.

My card was the Magician.

We spoke briefly before parting, agreeing to aid each other in times of need, since many of us feared persecution from our leaders. The Italian, of course, had a list of all the family surnames, but bid those amongst us to keep our own family history.

I already have such a history here in this book, and will keep record here of any happenings which may include this cadre of families. Someday the book will be the property of my son, and his generations thereafter.

The fact that the book had survived led me to believe that he had sent it with his cousin and son when they fled England after the failed attempt on Parliament. I read for another hour, which brought me up to the end of the 18th century. I stood up from the table and stripped off the gloves, closed the acid-free four-flap box, and started downstairs for a snack.

I shuddered as I caught the image of David's room out of the corner of my eye.

I was halfway through a bowl of Fruit Loops when my father walked through the door. His eyes were glazed over, and he laid his hand on the kitchen counter to steady himself.

"You alright?" I asked with my mouth full.

He looked up at me as if he was surprised by my presence. "What? Oh, yes, I'm fine ..."

He definitely wasn't. And the last thing I needed was for him to come off the spool right now before reinforcements arrived. I swallowed my cereal. "So, um, I may have some good news."

He looked at me, interested, but didn't speak.

"I, ah, I may have convinced Aria to show up for the alignment. Under the condition that we never bother her again."

That seemed to shake him awake, and a broad grin spread over his face. "It's all coming together, Zora. All the work, so many years, after all this time, it's going to work out. I can feel it."

"Don't get too excited," I warned him. I didn't want to sound overly-excited myself. I had to play this all just right. "She might change her mind yet, but ..."

"She'll come." He seemed so sure that it was making me nervous, wondering if he'd figured out what I was planning and had a counterplan already in place somehow. "And that will make four Arcana at least ..."

"What do you mean four?" My heart thudded against my ribs. What was he on about?

"It's meant to be, Zora! Don't you see?" He had this crazed look on his face, and it was seriously starting to freak me out. "I was reaching for a pen to sign a rental agreement on the property I found today—it's just perfect for the ceremony—and look!"

He reached into the interior pocket of his blazer.

And pulled out the Devil Card.

Chapter 15

I stared at the Card. And even though I knew the answer, I asked, "Did you find that in David's room?"

"No, Zora. I didn't find it. It found me."

My blood ran cold. "So does that mean you're the Devil *and* the Magician?" I literally could not think of a worse combination.

"I don't know yet. Perhaps. I haven't tried to connect with it yet, but … this is wonderful news!" He looked up from the Card to me, and the crazed expression terrified me.

Was there a way to keep him from communing with that Card? I didn't think so. Not if the Card had chosen him. I should have known that burying the Card with David wouldn't work. Lia's Card had been buried with her grandmother, and it appeared to her a generation later. Apparently, the Devil wasn't as patient.

Maybe I could at least distract him for a little while. Probably not more than a few hours, but at least that was a few hours that the deity energy of the Devil Card wouldn't be worming around in his brain. I had a pretty strong sense that Coyote wouldn't be the face of the energy that appeared to my desperate and power-mad father.

"Not to veer off-topic," I began, "but I've been reading the family history. I was gobsmacked when I read about Robert Catesby."

Dad's grin grew even wider, cementing his belief in my unwavering loyalty. "Yes! Wasn't that a shock?"

"So why did we avoid Bonfire Night then? I mean, we lived in the virtual epicenter of a holiday honoring our ancestor ..."

"Psh! Guy Fawkes gets all the credit with most people, even if they know the true history. That whole festival is a mockery of what Robert Catesby stood and died for."

"Okay, but mockery is kind of what the English do best, yeah? It still honors his ideas ..."

"It most certainly does not. It celebrates a criticism of power. But Catesby had so much more than that in his heart. He wanted to bring *change*, real change, not criticism. He was willing to give his own life to attempt to stop the oppression. Even if the plan had failed, which it did, ultimately, he was hoping it would galvanize others to stand up to the corrupt leaders!" Dad's fervor on this topic was a little alarming. How did he manage to avoid bringing this up in conversation for my whole life?

"We're not even Catholic, though ..." It was a weak protest, but I wanted to keep him talking.

"Ach, don't you see? Persecution of Catholics was just one example. It's about corruption in leadership! Back then it was hanging people of different faiths, but is it really any different now? Politicians in every country are no less corrupt than they were 400 years ago. They start wars, they lie to the public, they engage in back-room deals, and why? For the good of their own people? Of course not! It's to line their own dirty pockets! Think of the possibilities if the Arcana could band together for the good of humankind!"

"That's assuming the Arcana are good people, of course."

"Well, naturally," he continued, "there would have to be some sort of checks and balances within our number. And you're right, of course. Catesby himself found that out, or rather his son did."

"How do you mean?" I filled a glass with lemonade and set it in front of my father, trying to keep that I'm-on-your-side vibe so he'd expose all of the machinations of his reasoning. He was pretty excited to let it all spill, and the more information I had, the better armed I was to stop him.

"Ah. Cheers." He sipped his beverage and smiled at its sweetness. "Well, young Robert—I don't believe they used the term 'junior' back in those days—fled in the days before his father died, and the book was clearly sent with him."

"Yeah, I'm following so far."

"Where would he and his aunt—well, second cousin or something—have gone? Running to family or friends would have been easy to track, even then, and would have put their relations in danger."

"Certainly."

"If you read some of Robert the Younger's notes, it becomes clear that they tried to shelter with some of the Arcana families that were in-country. After all, an oath had been sworn amongst them, and Robert, though only a child, was likely to become the Magician in what was perhaps the very first hand-over of a Card since they were created."

"And they turned him away? Those were the 'neighbors' he mentioned in the journal?"

"Indeed. So you are correct, even within our ranks there are vipers who care only for themselves. They abandoned our family from the very outset."

I was beginning to understand his twisted logic. "But if we ARE family, then there's minimal risk of betrayal." Bloody hell. I almost felt guilty. Almost.

"Precisely! Families should work together, even if they disagree. So the more of us there are, the better. And then, in time, perhaps the entire

Arcana can be reunited now that no one's burning witches anymore. Or Catholics. Or whatever. You understand my meaning."

There was a point that was nagging at me, but I couldn't find a way to ask: had he known Rhys's mother was Arcana? "So one day, like twenty-two years ago, you just got the idea to start a magic family?" I tried to word the statement without judgement.

He took a long drink of his lemonade as he thought over his reply. "Well, my girl, as you know, I became the Magician when I was about your age. My father'd passed on, and I had no siblings, so the honor fell to me. Father had been preparing me my whole life, knowing that one day I'd inherit the Card. It was a strict upbringing, learning the family history, studying arcane magic, researching the whereabouts of the other Arcana families. I tried not to make things as strict on you. In any case, my father had started that research when he bought the country house at Lewes that you know so well."

"He had the idea?"

"Not the mechanism, no. But he had the dream of uniting the Arcana and restoring our family's former glory and place of respect. We'd lost all the holdings we had in Warwickshire, of course, and it took centuries to truly recover socially and financially. I suspect there was a part of him that wanted to create factions within the Arcana, based on the predisposition toward loyalty, but that seemed too esoteric a goal for me."

"Go on. Why have you never told me any of this?"

"Well, if I'm honest, there are some parts of my younger years that don't reflect very well on my character. At the risk of being indelicate, let me just say that in my twenties, I was a bit of a nomad. My father was gone, I had inherited his money and the powers of the Card, and I was eager to be free of the shackles he kept on me. I traveled around a good bit, and was, I confess, a bit of a hedonist with my newfound freedoms. In the US, no one knew me, and my accent and abilities opened a lot of doors. I could, quite literally have anything and anyone I wanted."

"And that wasn't enough?"

"For a time, it was. But by my late twenties, the shine was off the apple, you might say. I found myself out West, surrounded by all sorts of debauchery, and feeling empty. I met a young woman who captivated me, and I couldn't even tell you why. She wasn't more beautiful, or intelligent, or exciting than any of the others I'd met, but I felt connected to her. Even after we'd parted ways, I couldn't stop thinking of her. Or, rather, about how I felt during our short time together. It made me realize that I was wasting my life on foolishness. So I went home to Lewes and started taking my role as the Magician more seriously. I had several ideas of ways to bring the Arcana together, and actually considered starting a corporation so I could seek out Arcana families and start hiring them to work together in some global enterprise."

"That seems a lot easier than fathering a handful of children and hoping they'll inherit powers. No offense meant."

"No, no," he nodded fervently, "you're absolutely right. But that wouldn't create that connection, would it? Employees, even business partners, can walk away fairly easily. And it would be no less empty or lonely than my life had already become. But a family? Now that would be something! There have been historical dynasties that have spanned centuries! *That* was what I wanted."

I stared hard at him, feeling like I was seeing my father for the first time. The veneer was stripped away, and this was the authentic article, or at least it had been at one time. I had to remind myself that this vulnerable, idealistic, and probably misguided young man had been warped by obsession.

As if on cue, Dad reached into the cutlery drawer and pulled out a paring knife. He made a quick poke at his left thumb and rubbed the resulting drop of blood across the Devil Card.

My whole body tensed as I saw his crown chakra spring to life and a massive aura erupt around him. I'd seen something similar before when Aria called on her Goddess in my presence, but the intensity of the bonding process made this different. It was as though an eight-foot shadow stood behind my father, and though it was featureless, I got a good look at the shape as it turned its head to survey the surroundings into which it had been summoned. The body was clearly humanoid, but the head was definitely not. It resembled an odd mix of a dog and an anteater. Maybe a giraffe. Tess and Darcy flattened their ears and slipped around the kitchen island to stand behind me.

This was no Coyote, ready to play some pranks and wreak some havoc. I knew that shape from the Egyptian mythology I'd read as a child—a shape associated with chaos, violence, and wickedness.

My father's spirit had summoned Set.

This was bad.

Very bad.

Chapter 16

My father shivered with the rush of new power, then gazed at me with feverish eyes.

"Zora, my dear, I think I may go take a little time to myself, if you don't mind. I've enjoyed our conversation, but ..." He lifted the Devil Card and held it up as the shadow of Set absorbed itself into its new host. Dad's crown chakra pulsed erratically, and I figured there might be some conflict as two deities now inside him fought for dominance.

I nodded and kept my face neutral, but fear spread through me. "I might make a run to the store," I said calmly. "Do you need anything?"

"Not that I can think of." All he wanted right now was to get away from me and immerse himself in his newfound power. "Do let me know if you hear from your sister, though." He started walking toward his room, and I had a feeling I'd need to get my plan together very quickly.

"Before you go disappearing for the evening, what would you think about me driving down to St. Augustine to see if I can convince Lia to come back for a few days?"

He stopped in his tracks and turned to face me, wide-eyed. He strode back and wrapped me in a very brief but strong bear hug. "I'm so proud of how you're taking on so much to help this work. I know it can't be easy for you after what happened to David. It means the world to me to have you solidly on board."

I sputtered for words, but all I managed was, "No worries." I wasn't used to physical affection from him at all, and my impending betrayal twisted my stomach. My heart chakra twinged in complaint, but then my father spun on his heel and disappeared through his bedroom door without another word. The dogs made no attempt to follow.

I stared after him for a minute, and I couldn't help wondering if a war of wills was about to take place inside him. Up to now, my father had always been aligned to Mercury, the Roman god equivalent to the Greek god Hermes, more or less. I'll grant you, he'd leaned into Mercury's darker side, less about communication and more about manipulation.

How would Mercury and Set get along? I suspected not very well, since at their essence they were opposites. Mercury liked control; Set liked chaos. They both wanted power. Add to that the fact that I was pretty certain that my father was the first person ever to possess two Arcana titles at the same time, and this might well be a recipe for disaster.

I also wasn't sure what Set's powers were, but he was a master of deception, if memory served me right, and that might mean he'd see right through my false front once he and Dad fully bonded. That might represent real danger for me.

Especially now that Dad had realized that killing one of his own children would likely default that Card's powers directly to him. The father I knew wouldn't hurt me, but if his spirit had summoned a god as violent and devious as Set, that changed things. All bets were off.

For the first time in my life, I felt genuinely unsafe.

I needed to get out of here right away.

***

I texted Rhys as I threw a small duffel bag together with a couple of outfits, some toiletries, a phone charger, and the few genuinely sentimental possessions I owned: a locket with my mother's picture on one side and mine on the other which my mother had worn until the day she was buried, a quartz pendant inlaid with semiprecious stones representative of each chakra which I had bought for myself with my Christmas money when I was eighteen, and a small box of photos I had nicked from my mother's and father's larger collections. Any other possessions I had were just *things*, and I wouldn't miss them if I could never come back for some reason.

Once my bag was packed, I snagged my car keys and fled to the garage where my sedan was parked. There was a lump in my throat as I tossed my bag in the boot, thinking about how the last time I'd driven in this car, David had been riding shotgun.

My eyes filled with tears, and I ran back in the house and up the stairs, knowing Dad wouldn't be coming out to say good-bye. For the first time since he died, I found myself in the room which had briefly been Aria's and then David's. His belongings were still scattered all over. I reached down and scooped up a handful of the Pokémon cards he'd stolen and clutched them to my chest. I wanted something of his with me.

A cool breeze blew across my right arm, and I spun around searching for what had caused the shift in the air.

Except for me, the room was empty.

Swallowing hard, I bolted out the door and back to my waiting car. I tucked the cards into the side pocket of my duffel, slammed the boot shut, and slid into the driver's seat, my heart pounding in my throat.

I sent Dad a text saying that I didn't want to waste any time in case Lia needed convincing, and that I was heading for Florida. He didn't respond, but I didn't really expect him to.

He probably couldn't hear me over the two gods arguing in his head.

***

Rhys and I met up at a fast-food restaurant a few miles away. He stared at me over a strawberry milkshake.

"I'm glad you got out of there," he said. He pinched the bridge of his nose as he was assaulted by a brain freeze. "I'll feel a lot better knowing he—what do I call him? Dad?—can't konk you over the head or mind control you or anything."

"It was actually pretty terrifying. It's like I could see the wheels turning, thinking of all kinds of ways to get what he wants, no matter the cost."

"You did the right thing to try and convince him you were on his side."

"It wasn't hard to do," I admitted. "Probably because, as far as he knows, I've never lied to him. And I was telling him what he wanted to hear, so there's that. I felt like a right chiseler, even though I knew it was the smart thing to do."

"A right what now?"

"A right chiseler. Con artist."

"Oh. Haven't heard that one before." He took another slurp of his milkshake. "Should you maybe talk to Aria before you head down to Florida? Make sure she's got Lia's stamp of approval?"

"Yeah, I suppose I'd better. She might not have talked to her yet; it's only been a few hours."

I shot Aria a text asking if she'd spoken to Lia, and then grumpily dipped a french fry in my own milkshake. Chocolate, though, not strawberry. That'd be grotesque on a fry.

Summer vacation was winding down for both of my sisters ... Aria would be entering her junior year, while Lia was a year older and would be a senior. I couldn't help wondering if maybe there was even another one of Dad's offspring somewhere between Lia and me, given the four years between us.

"So listen," Rhys began. "I feel like I should tell you that I called my mom this morning after you went back to the house and told her everything. She's absolutely beside herself about the whole thing."

"Why? She didn't do anything wrong."

"No, but she's just blown away by how messed up this all is. And even though she's never met you, she's desperately worried about *my three sisters*. It blew her mind, honestly. She said she'd drive up to St. Augustine to meet Lia's family if it would help."

"Your mom sounds really nice." My heart hurt a little, missing my own mother who, while *nice* might not have always been the right word for her, would never have let Dad put me in danger if she had known. "I don't know if it would help or not, but maybe just having a Gen-Xer on site would make Lia's family feel a little bit better. I haven't had any contact with her in eight months."

"Well, it's not a far drive, only an hour and a half. So you have a little time to decide. Do you ..." he hesitated, suddenly unsure of himself, "... want me to go with you to see her?"

I realized at that moment that I'd taken for granted that he'd be coming with me. Funny how I'd learned to depend on him so easily in just a few days. "I really would. You have such a calming influence on people, and, well, I know you have my back. I don't think I ever understood what an important feeling that is." I felt a tingle pass through me, and it took me a second to realize that it was Shakti's stamp of approval.

"Cool." He grinned sheepishly, and it was clear he'd been hoping I'd say yes. "Should we take both cars?"

"I don't really think it's necessary to take Priscilla, no offense—I'm thinking about the petrol costs—but where could you park her while we're gone?"

"Oh, I could park her at the church. I've made friends with the pastor there and have been doing some gardening for them in exchange for being able to use their bathroom and take up a parking spot."

My jaw dropped mid-french fry. "How did you manage to convince them to go along with that?"

He affected the worst English accent I'd ever heard. "I'm bloody charming, that's how."

My laughter started as a chuckle, then built to something near to hysteria. I had tears running down my face and could barely breathe. It was contagious, apparently, because Rhys started guffawing, too, and pretty soon, the restaurant staff was giving us a bombastic side-eye. It's not even that what he said was that funny; it was just that there was a lightness in my heart I hadn't felt in—well, ever.

After what seemed like several minutes, but was probably only three or four, my phone buzzed. I tried breathing deeply, unsure of which of my family members might be reaching out. To my relief, it was Aria. She texted to say that she had spoken to Lia, and while they both still had reservations, Lia was willing to speak to me as Aria had done. She wanted me to call in a couple of hours, after her mother would be home from work.

Things were looking up. Maybe.

***

Rhys gathered a few essentials out of Priscilla and we dropped the conversion van off at the church, then jumped on I-75 headed south. No reason not to keep moving toward our destination while we waited. Rhys called his mother, and she agreed to meet us in St. Augustine that evening.

The conversation with Lia went much the way the conversation with Aria had gone. Aria had already given her the backstory, but it was up to me to do the convincing that I wasn't making a second attempt at kidnapping and mayhem.

"Why should I even care about this? Seems to me like this is a *you* problem."

"It might be, except that he may well have figured out how to tap into your powers from a distance. At least if we're all united, we might be able to give some genuine resistance."

"You might have convinced Aria, but I don't see why I should trust anything you say." It was exasperating, but I couldn't really blame her for doubting my intentions.

"I really am sorry about how things went before. I've got a lot to answer for, and I get that. But we're under a bit of a time crunch."

"Again, not sure why that's a *me* problem. Why would I give you another chance to tie me up and turn me over to our psycho of a sperm donor?" Her tone and choice of words reminded me of David, and my heart ached.

"You absolutely don't have to meet with me alone or in private. I want to do anything I can to reassure you that I mean you no harm." The words *this time* were implied.

In the end, Lia, her mother Maddie, and her best friend Treigh agreed to speak to us when we arrived. To put them at ease, Rhys suggested a public location, and we agreed to meet up at a Mexican restaurant near Lia's house.

My stomach was full of butterflies. My behavior last year when Lia and I had first met was reprehensible. Just like with Aria, I had threatened her safety and her freedom. I expressed my concerns to Rhys as we drove.

"What if I can't make her not despise me? I don't want my sisters to hate me, but can I blame them?" Tears pricked the backs of my eyes, clouding my vision just slightly as I drove. I was grateful that I-75 was one long, boring shot.

"You have to show them that who they met is not who you are," Rhys answered sagely. "You were basically brainwashed. That's not an excuse, but it's a reason. We all just have to get through this week, and then you can start really trying to mend fences."

I was glad he didn't try to write off the horrible things I'd done. I had a lot to answer for, even if I had been heavily influenced.

Rhys was right. The first priority was to stop our father, and only then could I try to build any sort of relationship with either of the girls.

I truly, deeply hoped I'd get the chance to make things right.

Chapter 17

"This might be a rude question, but is there really no deity that aligns itself with The Fool?" It was a question that had been nagging me since he first told me what Card he carried.

"Like I told you, mostly I just tap into my Higher Self, which gives me really good intuition and stuff. I am aligned with a deity, but he's not, you know, *involved*. You have to think about what The Fool represents, not its name."

"Which is?"

"At the core, The Fool represents new beginnings, curiosity, freedom, and innocence. But with that—and I hate to admit that I'm a bit guilty of more than one of these—comes impulsivity, being pretty dense about others' feelings, obsessing about stuff, and acting without considering consequences. There are quite a few deities who might align with some combination of those things, actually. Deities of travel, learning, nature—depends on the person."

"How about you, then?"

"My deity is Meili. He's Norse. Sort of a god of wanderlust, I guess."

"Well, that's definitely on-brand." I hazarded a quick glance away from the road to smirk at him.

"I suppose it is," Rhys smiled back. "He kind of swoops in from time to time when I'm on some new adventure, but He doesn't *guide* me per se, and I don't ask Him anything. Sometimes I'll get a sense of *thumbs-up* or *thumbs-down* about something. That's kind of what happened when I headed to Atlanta. I got the impulse to go, but I was having a really nice time on the beach, and wanted to chill for a few more days. Meili gave me a fly-by *thumbs-down* to that idea, so I packed my gear and started driving. I figure if He felt like it was important enough for a visit, I'd better listen. How about you?"

Even though Rhys had just freely shared his divine association, I felt nervous about sharing back. I'd never talked to anyone about Shakti. Dad knew She was my goddess, but that was all. He never asked about how we communicated. He seemed content to know what my powers were. Still, it only seemed fair for me to pay Rhys back in kind. Trust had to start somewhere. Why not with a Fool?

"Mine is the Hindu goddess Shakti. She's the embodiment of feminine energy. So, like, she can be any of the other goddesses, because they're all part of her."

"That sounds sort of confusing."

"Not really, when you consider that all divine energy is from the same source. Just different facets of the same jewel, She says." I shrugged. Hinduism has literally millions of gods, and I certainly wasn't an expert on most of them.

"How does She communicate with you?"

"For clear communication, I have to meditate. It's better if my chakras are in balance, too."

"You said that's one of your powers. I know a little about them because my mom taught me how to do Reiki healing. You have to know a little about the aura and chakras to do that."

I nodded. "I can see other people's chakras and the energy fluctuations within them. Makes it pretty hard to lie to me, for one. And I can tell when Arcana are using their deity's powers because the crown chakra lights up. I can see deity auras, too. That's how I knew what god Dad had summoned when he bonded with the Devil Card. I recognized Set's shadow from mythology books."

"That's a pretty handy trick."

"Handier still that Dad doesn't know I can do it."

"How'd you manage to hide that one?"

"I don't know, I guess it just never came up. Until recently, the only Arcanas I'd been around were Dad and Mum, and they'd never invoked their deities around me. So I didn't even realize I could do it until I met Aria."

"Not with Lia?"

"We didn't directly interact much; it was more Dad. She never called her deity around me, so I never had the chance. I presume it's some moon deity or another. But Aria's is definitely Egyptian, and based on the spectral scales she can also summon, my bet goes to Ma'at, Egyptian goddess of truth."

"That seems appropriate for Judgement."

"Yeah, and I'll tell you, when she summoned those scales in front of me, it shook me to my knickers."

"How so?" He turned toward me, fascinated.

"I don't know how to explain it exactly, but the sight of those scales laid my own crimes bare. All the things I'd been justifying for Dad's reasons ... well, all my excuses were ripped away. I could feel in my bones the wrong I'd done. I think that's what broke whatever mind control Dad might have been using on me. It was the scariest thing I ever felt. Like she had the power to end me right there."

"End you? Like kill you? She sounded mad, but not homicidal ..."

"No, not kill me, I guess. But I felt real danger, real power. And she knew how to use it, too. I'm betting she would have if I had reacted the wrong way. I'm also betting that's why Dad let her leave. If she pulled those out on him ..."

"He's got a lot more to answer for than you do."

"And if she laid that out on him like she did to me, he'd have been freaking terrified. That's a lot of power for an angry 15-year-old to have. Who knows what she'd have been able to do to him."

"This might sound cold-hearted, but I think I'm pretty glad for that right about now." He leaned back in his seat and stretched. "And as for you, I think I get why Shakti is your deity."

"How do you mean?" I wasn't sure I liked being analyzed, but I was interested in his assessment.

"Well, when people think of strength, they think of physical strength, right? Like Hercules or something. But physical strength has its limits. Strength of mind, though, that has *no* limits. Strength to endure, strength to do the hard things, strength to love and trust when you've been manipulated and hurt your whole life...that's you. And from what you said, that's Shakti. The essence of *woman* is internal strength."

"And you think that's me?"

"Of course it is, Zora. You're the lynchpin for this whole rag-tag family. No one else could have done what had to be done to bring us together. Only you."

"I certainly don't feel like Strength right now. I feel like a total failure."

"And yet you don't give up. How easy would it be to just say, 'the hell with it all' and disappear? But you're not. You're pushing through the pain and the shame and the grief to try and do the right thing. To try and protect your family, even if they don't like you. I *do* like you, by the way."

His words squeezed my heart, and I was glad to be looking at the road so that he wouldn't see that tear running down my left cheek.

***

By the time we got to Nacho Taco in St. Augustine, the late Florida summer sun was casting long shadows across the parking lot as it began to set. Ellen Baker was waiting for us, leaning against the back of a several-years-old red Prius. Her face lit up when Rhys emerged from the passenger side of my car. I slid a pack of David's pokemon cards in my back pocket. Oddly, I felt that he should be here for this.

I'm not sure what I was expecting a former Arcana to look like, but Ellen wasn't it. She was sporting wildly patterned yoga pants, an explosion of teal, pink, and orange, and an almost-the-same-shade teal tee shirt with FLORIDA emblazoned above a cartoon of a couple of manatees. Her ashy blond hair was thrown into a messy bun. The grin, though...I'd seen it a dozen times on Rhys's face, and it looked just as comfortable on hers.

"Hey, Bubs." She threw her arms around her son and squeezed.

"Hey, Ma," he gasped as she squished the air out of him. He hugged her back and kissed the top of her head.

A tick of the clock, and she turned her eyes to me. "You must be Zora. Rhys told me what was happening. I'm so sorry for what you're going through." She moved to hug me, but must have picked up on the tension that rippled through my whole frame, so she grabbed my hands and held them between hers instead. "You've been through so much."

She looked me over, almost as though she was searching for an injury, and I saw the faint flare of her chakras, and her third eye pulsed a deep violet. Interesting. Apparently, I could even see the chakras of former Arcana. "Oh, my dear, your aura is a mess." She started scraping the air around me as though scooping mud off my shoulders.

"Ma, I don't think a parking lot is the right place to be scraping her aura. Plus she just met you. You're gonna freak her out." Rhys's words may have been critical, but his voice was filled with affection.

Ellen shot him a sidelong glance. "Psh. I'm sure she's used to worse."

"Not from total strangers." He was trying not to laugh, I could tell.

"Mm, maybe not. Still, you should have done this for her already. Honestly, Rhys, she's got the weight of the world on her. How's she supposed to think clearly with ..."

"It's okay, really," I began, not sure what to say to interrupt this bizarre conversation. "Rhys has been a huge support."

"I'm so glad." That warm smile spread across her face again. "I just can't believe that Dorian has orchestrated such an intricate mess. I knew he was intense, but ..." She shrugged, and I could see where her son got his signature move.

"Did you know he was an Arcana, Ma?"

Her eyes grew far away, like she was reaching back for a memory. "I don't know. I might have. To be completely honest, I don't remember a lot of that weekend. There was this crazy rave in Santa Fe ..." Her smile widened, and I was pretty sure I didn't want to know what she was remembering. Fortunately, she didn't share. "Anyway, I must have thought something of him if I took his picture with my dad's old camera. I didn't use the Polaroid that much. That was old, even then. But I took pictures of special people and places so I'd have a concrete memory. So I must have known he was special. When I turned up pregnant, I knew right away where this little nugget came from." She let go of my hands and squished Rhys's cheeks between her palms.

"Alright, Ma," he laughed, pulling her hands away. "How about we go get a seat and wait for Lia?"

***

We settled ourselves at a large table in the corner of the palm-thatch-covered outdoor patio and the server brought us glasses of water and a basket of chips and salsa. It wasn't long before Lia, her mother Maddie, and her best friend Treigh strode through the double doors that led to the interior of the restaurant. The server pointed them toward our table and they took a collective breath before moving toward us.

They were a motley crew to be sure. Maddie Alvarez looked like a beautiful suburban mom in her neatly-pressed French blue blouse and khaki capris. Treigh looked like something out of a cologne ad in his designer casual wear and fancy sunglasses. And Lia looked like a glam-goth princess, sporting a red and black tank top under a fishnet crop-top tee, black-on-black brocade leggings, and a pair of black Doc Martens. Her hair was a legendary dye job of vertical red and black stripes. The make up she wore was far more elaborate than I'd ever seen it, with delicate red and black shading and eyeliner coming to needle-like points at the ends of perfectly-painted wings. The inner corners extended slightly down the bridge of her nose. Her lips were a fascinating gradient of red and black.

Her crown chakra was pulsing softly, and I wondered what deity power she was using..

I stood, suddenly deeply unsure of myself. "Thank you for coming," I stammered out. "This is Rhys and his mother Ellen."

Rhys jumped up and extended his hand, and I saw Treigh tense for action. His posture relaxed when he realized Rhys wasn't a threat.

Lia scanned Rhys up and down before extending her own hand in response. "So you're my brother?"

There was that infectious grin, spreading across his face again. "Apparently I'm the first of the litter." That brought a tiny smile to her heavily-tinted lips. "Killer makeup," he added.

"War paint," she replied, but she didn't sound angry. "The hair is a glamour." I guess that answered my question about the power.

There was a second of awkward silence, then Maddie spoke up. "Why don't we sit down so we can hear what everyone has to say?" We all complied, and she leaned across the table, locking eyes with me. "I'm not going to pull any punches here. You endangered my daughter, and I'm disinclined to go along with literally anything you say. I've only agreed to this much because Lia persuaded me that this is a much bigger issue than just what happened here last fall. Let me make one thing clear, though. My daughter isn't going anywhere without me."

"Or me," Treigh spoke up. He crossed his arms and I detected a deliberate flex of his pectorals and biceps to make his point. He'd rescued her from us once, and he wasn't going to allow her to be hurt.

I took a deep breath, knowing that this showdown would come. "Whatever anger you have toward me is totally justified," I began. I had rehearsed this speech in my head for the better part of an hour. "I can't and won't try to excuse the part I had in misleading and snatching Lia. There's not even a good defense except to say that I was being manipulated to believe I was doing the right thing. Still, I should have been able to see through it, and I'm deeply sorry for what we put you through."

Maddie raised an arched eyebrow at me and leaned back. "Well, you've certainly inherited your father's silver tongue." I couldn't tell if that was an insult, but it felt like one.

Rhys jumped to my defense. "It's more than that," he said quietly. "That's part of his power. Plus, he'd been grooming her to trust him blindly for years. He isolated her from friends and outsiders. He made her feel like all they had was each other. He treated her like his most trusted sidekick. What kid wouldn't have blind loyalty to her father after that, at least for a while?"

My eyes about bugged out of my head as he spoke. I didn't expect him to speak for me at all, certainly not with such fervor. Ellen reached out and patted his hand proudly.

Lia's cadre seemed to consider this. "So y'all just met?" she asked him.

"Yeah, a couple of weeks ago. The Universe drew me to her. She didn't find me; it was the other way around."

"Is that one of your powers?"

"Sort of, yeah. I know where I need to be if it's important."

"And Dorian doesn't know about you?" Maddie broke in. "How is that possible?"

Ellen shrugged and spread her palms. "I had a wild youth. I only knew Dorian for a weekend. I didn't even know his last name."

Maddie nodded, appraising Ellen, who was clearly younger than she was, even though Rhys was older than Lia. Maddie had been a young professional when Dad met and wooed her.

"So what is it you want from me, exactly, and why should I care?" There was a flash across Lia's heart chakra, and despite her toughness, I could tell that she was sympathetic to what Dad had put us all through, even me. I also noticed that she wouldn't look directly at me.

"I can't be sure of this, but I'm beginning to suspect that Dad's plan is less about forming some sort of Arcana committee and more about taking some of our powers for himself through this ritual. He says he wants to bind us together, and at first I thought he meant that metaphorically, but now I think maybe he's figured out how to use our bloodline to feed our powers to him. Especially now that he knows that if one of us dies, he might end up with their Card ..." There was a lump in my throat as I thought of David.

"When he came into possession of the Devil Card, he summoned a very dangerous and wicked deity to him," Rhys offered, seeing that I needed a moment to recover.

"Explain to me again why no one called the police," Treigh insisted from behind his fancy Ray Bans.

I did my best to explain, but even to my own ears, it sounded weak. Like I was just trying to protect my own hide. Lia barely glanced at me the whole time, as if what was happening on the other side of the patio was more interesting.

"This is outrageous," Maddie announced when I finished. "Someone needs to answer for that boy's death, and I frankly don't care if it's Dorian or you."

"David says Zora tried to look out for him," Lia said quietly.

Everyone fell silent, and I felt a chill creep down my back. I touched my back pocket where the Pokémon cards were. David was *here?* And Lia could see him?

"He says what he did was dumb, but that it's our father's fault. He says Zora is trying to do what's right."

Rhys's eyes filled with tears. "David's here?"

Lia nodded. "He says Zora told him to stay with her after he died, that she didn't want him to be alone and angry."

I felt myself trembling. "Kid," I whispered, but then my words were drowned by the tears that slid down my cheeks. Rhys put his arm around me, and I could feel him shaking, too. Ellen's eyes pooled up as she witnessed our grief.

Even Lia's lips were trembling, her eyes red. "He says our father has to pay. That we don't have to like each other, but we have to stop Dorian Blair."

Chapter 18

That night, I lay awake on the futon in Ellen's front room, staring at the glow-in-the-dark stars on her ceiling. Her tiny bungalow was in the heart of the psychic community of Cassadaga, Florida, which is really a town called Lake Helen if you want to be fussy about it. It was well dark when we drove in, but there were several residents out for evening walks, even at this late hour. Soaking in the moonlight, Ellen told me.

Truth be told, Ellen's house was only slightly larger than Priscilla, but to someone who spent most of her life living in vans or RVs, it was probably spacious enough. There was one bedroom, one bathroom, and a front room which encompassed the living, dining, and kitchen space. It was smaller than any apartment I'd ever been in. Had it not been built in 1930, I suspect you could have called it one of those tiny houses that were so popular these days.

Still, the feel of it was nice and cozy. Like Ellen herself, the place was decorated in bright colors, but instead of looking chaotic and crazy, it all sort of blended together in a Bohemian vibe that made me feel like I was in a gift shop.

With only the nearly-full moon casting its muted glow through the thin curtains, the colors were softer and dreamier, and my mind drifted like lily pads on a pond.

I closed my eyes and found myself on the mental island where I met with Shakti. Much to my surprise, she was already there waiting for me.

"Hello, Zora. You've been very busy, my dear."

"I have, yeah. Tonight went better than I figured it would. Lia's going to head to Atlanta tomorrow." With her mom and Treigh in tow, of course.

"You are bringing your siblings together. This is a good thing." She was wearing the aspect I recognized as Durga. Big mom energy. Nine of her ten hands were peacefully folded in her lap, and the other was absently petting her lioness, who was knocked out snoozing beside her on the picnic table.

"Lia saw David." My heart chakra flared and then quieted. The knowledge that the kid was following me around and not stuck in some empty building made me feel good. I was also relieved that he wasn't mad at me.

Shakti nodded. "This is also good. Perhaps you will be able to help his spirit find peace."

"Knowing him, peace isn't quite what he's after." I sat on the bench beside her, and we both looked out at the water. Several bright lights from the sky mirrored themselves on the surface. "It looks different here tonight."

"The alignment approaches," she stated simply, and one of her arms made a sweeping gesture toward the sky. "You were right to flee your father, Zora. The two divine energies within him are volatile and dangerous."

"Will I be able to stop him?"

"Not by yourself, but with all of you together, there is a chance. You must explore your powers before the ritual. You have but scratched the surface. There is much to learn."

"Can't you just tell me what to do?"

She shot me some side-eye. "Your powers are not parlor tricks, Zora. They come from within you. The energy of the chakras is the energy of the Universe. It connects us to all that is, including each other. How that will manifest itself is a product of your spirit, not My power. You have not properly studied how you might make use of your command of the chakras. Part of that is your father's doing, because he sought to temper your light. Unfortunately, that means you must be a fast student now."

I wanted to complain, but I knew she was right. She was giving me the straightest answer She could. "I'm scared I'll fail," I admitted.

"I believe in you," She replied, and then we just sat in silence, gazing at the lights in the water and listening to the sounds of a snoring lion.

***

S peaking of snoring lions, I woke up with a tuxedo cat curled up against my right hip. When I stirred, it opened one green eye and extended a paw out to touch my ribs, as if encouraging me to sleep for a few more minutes. It was right tempting, I can't lie. But there was much to be done, and so the beast would have to settle for a bit of an ear scratching.

That seemed a satisfactory compromise, and it squinked its eyes at me.

I'd never had a cat, never even really thought about it, but waking up to cuddles was awfully comforting. Dad had never allowed the dogs to sleep in beds.

"Oh, Victoria, that's where you got off to last night!" Ellen bustled in wearing a brightly-colored caftan, her blond hair a wild cloud around her head. "You should consider yourself privileged, Zora. She doesn't normally take to strangers right away. She must know you're family. Did you sleep well?"

"I did, thanks. I communed with my goddess, and then I guess I just drifted off after that."

"Ah, wonderful. Did your goddess have any insights on how to handle the next few days?" Ellen opened a small cabinet and pulled out a box of peppermint tea bags, then filled the kettle and turned on the small stove.

"She told me I needed to learn more about my abilities. I guess I can do more than read chakras and channel energy to lift stuff."

"Well, darling, if you can channel energy, I imagine you can do quite a lot. That's the basis for nearly all of what people call magic, wouldn't you agree?"

I sat up and blinked, eliciting a chuff of protestation from Victoria, who promptly yawned so widely that I thought she might unhinge her jaw. "What do you mean?"

Ellen sat on the side of the futon and the cat promptly abandoned me and settled in her lap. "Manipulation of energy is the basis for nearly every type of spiritual work. Healing, telekinesis, psychometry, even astral projection in its own way—they all involve manipulation of the electrical fields that run through each and every one of us. Have you never experimented with such things?"

"I guess it never occurred to me." I felt like a dolt. How had I made it eight years as an Arcana without pushing the limits of my powers to see what I could do?

"I suspect that was Dorian's doing," Ellen commented, patting my hand. It was as though she knew exactly what I was thinking. "I didn't know him for long, but he definitely struck me as someone who wants control of his world. Even if he'd stayed around, we wouldn't have worked out. I'm no good at being obedient."

"I wouldn't have thought I was, either. But here we are."

"You have a steep learning curve, but I can show you a few of the things I know, and then maybe you'll find a way to incorporate it into your own magic."

"Rhys never said anything about manipulating energy as one of his powers," I mused.

"That's because it isn't one of my powers." A yawning, stretching Rhys emerged from the back room just as the kettle began to whistle. He pulled three cups out of the cabinet and got our tea bags steeping. "At least it's not an Arcana power for me. It's an everybody-has-it power."

Ellen nodded. "Many people have the ability to work with energy. That's the basis for reiki, of course. We remove blockages in the body's energy pathways by releasing stress and anxiety, thus allowing the patient's natural processes to work to heal the body more efficiently."

"Rhys mentioned reiki. He said that's how he knew about chakras."

"Chakras aren't necessarily a part of reiki practice specifically, but if a reiki healer has a knowledge of them, they can be even more effective in their work, since chakras are focal points of energy."

"Maybe you should give her a reiki session," Rhys suggested.

"I think it might be more effective if we did it together," Ellen postulated. "Your powers might complement each other since you're connected by blood and power."

And so an hour later, I found myself flat on my back on a folding massage table with Rhys and his mother leaning over me. Soft, tinkly music was playing in the background and the scent of nag champa filled the air. I closed my eyes as Ellen hovered her hands over them. I focused on my crown chakra, imagining it as an amethyst, glowing a clear and radiant lavender. Her hands were so close to my skin that I could feel a gentle heat caressing my forehead.

After a couple of seconds, she moved her hands to frame my face, and the heat spread to my temples. It was peculiar, though, that even with her hands gone, I could still feel the warmth above my brows. When she brought her wrists together above my head, forming sort of a hand-hat on top of my locs, I felt a sensation akin to a sigh shudder through my whole aura.

I couldn't help it. I opened my eyes. But it wasn't the colorful room I saw, it was a swirling, moving mass of light and mist less than two inches from my face. It took me a mo to orientate myself, but then I realized what I was seeing: I was looking at my aura *from the inside.*

Ellen moved to her next position, and I shifted my focus to my third eye. It was as though I could feel the muscles between my eyes relaxing, expanding into a purple mist that joined my aura and began swirling about. As she moved to my side and her hands moved down to my solar plexus, Rhys stepped up and started the positions from the beginning, following after her by what might have been six or seven minutes. I wasn't too sure about the passage of time.

When Rhys's hands moved into the first position, I felt a deep tingle in my crown chakra and a string of lavender light flowed from my forehead like a glowing ribbon. The loose end snaked around in the air for a moment, then brushed along Rhys's crown chakra and attached itself. I heard Rhys gasp, and wondered if he could see the light or just feel it.

Rhys and his mother kept working their way down my body, and as Rhys hovered over each chakra, a different-colored ribbon of energy emerged and linked with his: violet, indigo, blue, green, gold, orange, and finally red. The final result, after what must have been 45 minutes, was a full rainbow of energy connecting us.

I knew when they were finally done, because Rhys broke the near-silence. "Well, that's something new."

"Can you see it?" I was afraid to move.

"A little bit, if I don't look directly. But I can sure feel it. It's like lying on top of a car hood while the engine is running." I thought that was a pretty good analogy.

"The air is certainly charged," Ellen said, her voice barely above a whisper. She held her hands up in front of her and closed her eyes. "I feel electricity pulsing back and forth. I think you're charging each other's spirit batteries."

It was a funny way to word what was happening, but it felt accurate. I slowly rose to a sitting position, and the rainbow wavered, but remained intact. If I was acting as a battery, maybe I was affecting Rhys's powers in more ways than a pretty light show. "Try using your powers, Rhys."

"My powers don't really work that way. They're more passive. Like I can sense the Pattern and I can't be mind-controlled. I don't have direct powers like being strong or creating illusions."

"Try making your natural protection against control into a shield," Ellen suggested. "Protection magic is one of the most useful skills energy-workers utilize. Imagine a transparent eggshell around you that protects you from control."

Rhys cocked his head to one side, then nodded and closed his eyes. Light seeped from the rainbow like dripping paint, blending together to create a pure, white glow which surrounded him like a second skin.

"Whoa," I muttered, and he half-smiled without opening his eyes. The rainbow rippled again, and a similar aura of white light enveloped me from head to toe. I could feel my skin tingling all over.

Rhys opened his eyes. "Did it work?"

"Heckin' yeah, it worked!" I looked at my hands and flexed them, feeling the energy pulse across my palms.

Ellen stepped up to Rhys and held her palm a couple of inches away from his skin. "Oh, my!" she exclaimed. "It appears that whatever you two did has enabled Rhys to create very powerful psychic shields around the both of you."

Rhys's eyes sparkled with excitement. "Do you think that if this works for the two of us that it would work on Lia and Aria, too?"

A slow smile spread across my face. For the first time since realizing I had to ruin Dad's ritual, I felt a sense of hope and purpose.

But more than that, I had a plan.

Chapter 19

I texted Dad that I'd been able to convince Lia to come, and after half an hour, I got a smile emoji and a thumbs-up emoji in return. That was ... atypical, and frankly, a bit worrisome. Emojis? Dad? My mind raced, wondering what this deity-battle was doing to my father's mind. I was certain it couldn't be good.

Rhys and I began the drive back to Atlanta, having confirmed with Lia that she would be making the trip with Treigh and her mother in tow. I couldn't really blame her for bringing reinforcements. I had chucked her into a van and tied her up in a vacation rental home, after all. Then I tried to run them off the road in order to rescue Dad from getting hauled off to the cops.

I'd been little better to Aria during her stay. No van-chucking per se, but I'd stood by while Dad convinced her Aunt Pam and cousin Logan to run off the road, and then convinced Logan to stay all zombie-like in our hotel room for a while. Then I stood by as she was coerced to come back to Atlanta with us.

It was a wonder that either of them were willing to even hear me out.

I let Rhys drive for part of the way so that I could think and plan. Knowing that I could connect my siblings' energy and create a shared conduit opened up all kinds of possibilities. I needed to talk to the girls to find out what exactly their abilities were so that I could maximize that skill.

My attention drifted, and I found myself staring at the blur of passing trees one minute, then looking at the tranquil waters around my meditation island the next. I hadn't tried to meditate, but my mind had brought me here nonetheless.

The strains of gentle stringed music floated on the air, and I approached the bridge where Shakti usually made her entrance. From the mists across the water, a shape emerged—not on the bridge, but floating in the water. The figure floated closer, and I was quite surprised to see my Goddess sitting in the center of a giant lotus, strumming a stringed instrument I didn't recognize.

"Well, that's a fine entrance," I commented, and she looked up with a smile. She looked a bit different from her usual appearance, too. Her sari was a gleaming white, and she only had four arms instead of the larger numbers I was used to seeing. It's like it was a simpler version of Her somehow. She wasn't even wearing jewelry, apart from a small white crescent-shaped bindi.

"You've called to a new part of Me today," she replied, her voice melodic and hypnotizing. "This aspect is Saraswati. I come to you this way because you are learning great things, Zora."

"Will this work, my plan?" I asked.

"You know I cannot tell you that, child. But your chances of success are much higher than they were when last we spoke."

"One thing I don't understand. I know that I have skill with chakras, but how is it the domain of Strength to do all this rainbow energy stuff?"

She looked at me and picked out a tune, and I knew she was waiting for me to answer my own question.

"It's because we're stronger together, isn't it?"

She winked at me, and even though I took it as confirmation, I was still a bit miffed to not get a straight answer.

As if reading my mind, she said, "True learning comes from you drawing conclusions from the facts you've learned, not from me telling you what to think."

I ground my teeth a little, but I knew she was right. She started to float back toward whatever reality lay on the far side of the bridge.

"Is that it, then? That's a pretty short convo."

"You have too much to do to spend your time in this place, my dear. But I will leave you with one thing to consider. You have many powers, as do your siblings, each according to your Cards. But remember this: You have the powers of the Cards that have followed your bloodlines, as does your father. But you all have something more than what he has, even separately. You not only have Strength's blood, The Fool's blood, Judgement's blood, and The Moon's blood ... you also each carry The Magician's blood within you. I think perhaps your father isn't taking that into account."

My jaw dropped as she sailed out of sight, the twang of her instrument fading into the distance.

***

When my mind returned to the here-and-now, I was alarmed to find Rhys singing Neil Diamond lyrics at a shocking volume.

"What if I'd been trying to sleep?" I groused.

"Sweeeet Caroliiiine ... dah dah dah ... !" The man would not be dissuaded from the mother of all sing-alongs. He glanced at me out of the corner of his eye as acknowledgement, but went right along with Neil for the whole rest of the song. At the end, he cranked the radio volume down a bit and sighed contentedly. "That song's one of the great joys in life, Zora."

"Yeah, yeah," I muttered, daring not to admit that under different circumstances, I'd spouted a verse or two myself.

"So were you communing with your Goddess or something?" I'm not sure why, but the fact that he was so unfazed by my being essentially unconscious and unreachable for however long it was—ten minutes? Thirty minutes? An hour? No way to know—brought me a sense of comfort. I'd never really been close to anyone but my parents, because who could explain all this weirdness to normal people?

"Yeah, Shakti had to drop some wisdom on me."

"What did She have to say to you? Must've been important."

"She reminded me that, in addition to our own inherited powers, we carry The Magician's blood as well."

"His blood but not his Card, though. What do you think is important about that?" Rhys bent his head from side to side, cracking his neck.

"I'm not sure, but She seemed to think it was significant that Dad hadn't figured on it being important, either."

Rhys was silent for a moment. "Maybe it's like some strange magical genetics. For most Arcana, they have a magical bloodline and a normal bloodline. But for us, there is no normal bloodline. Both halves have magical blood. That does seem important somehow, but I fail to see how that would affect our abilities."

I nodded. "Maybe it doesn't affect ours so much as it does *his*. As a general rule, it's harder to use skills against other Arcana members, right?"

"I've never really tried, but I've heard that, sure."

"So maybe he won't be able to use his mojo jojo on us as easily. He had a lot of trouble controlling Lia and Aria. No luck at all with David."

"And he really only managed to control you, I'll bet, because he'd basically brainwashed you for most of your life. So his control wasn't so much magical in your case as it was psychological."

As much as that stung, it was also true. "That might be useful if he tries mind-controlling us, but he already knows that it wasn't as effective as he'd hoped with the other kids."

"We need to meet up with the others and experiment with some of our skills before this ritual thing," he advised.

"You're right about that." I shifted in my seat because my butt was falling asleep. "Let me see if I can set something up."

I texted Aria, hoping she'd remember not to put anything in the text string that wasn't okay for Dad to see. I didn't know if he could access my texts, but he was the primary account holder on the phone plan, so it was possible. I couldn't believe I hadn't thought until now to get a burner phone. Bollocks.

Hey, Aria. R U on ur way?

There was a short pause before she responded. *Ya, we get in sometime tonight. We got a vacay rental.*

Nice. Can I call to discuss meeting up when we're all back in ATL?
Sure.

As much as my generation prefers text convo, talking was definitely safer in this situation. I rang her number and she picked up immediately.

"Any luck with Lia?" She got down to business right away.

"Yeah, she's on her way with her mom and bestie. Maybe you should call her. I have no idea where she's staying."

"I'll do that when I get off with you. So how are we going to handle this? I mean, do we all just look sternly at him and hope he'll see the light?" Sarcasm laced her voice.

"Actually, I've learned a few things that may help." I filled her in on what had happened during the reiki session and how the rainbow light show might allow us to strengthen and even combine our powers to some extent.

"To what end, though? Of all of us, I have the most reason to hate him. He's responsible for my parents' deaths. As much as I despise him, I don't think I could kill him."

"What do you mean, responsible for their deaths?" This was news to me. She explained how he had used his abilities to cloud the mind of the pilot on a small plane on which Amanda and Steven Rush had been traveling, causing him to misjudge his altitude and crash upon landing. I was gobsmacked. And given that he'd learned that the deaths of his kids might lead to his gaining their Cards and abilities, I was more anxious than ever.

"I think we all need to get together in order to test out what we can do if we're working together. Even with all he's done, I don't think I could kill him either. Maybe we can bind his powers or something?"

We brainstormed a few ideas, and then she signed off to call our other sister. Could we have done a three-way call? Sure. But I still felt right twitchy being around Lia because she hardly knew me at all. Or maybe it was just that I felt so guilty about tying her up like a rodeo calf. It might be that.

Aria called me back twenty minutes later to say that her lot would be flying into Atlanta at 4:00 that afternoon, and that Lia's group would be checking into their hotel around that same time. I looked at the clock in my car and figured we'd roll into town maybe an hour before they would. Of course, at that hour, it might take Aria and her Sheffield cousins a whole extra hour to get to their short-term vacation rental. Atlanta traffic is brutal.

We decided that staying at a nearby public location might be the smartest idea in case Dad was tracking my phone. I shot him a vague text about meeting folks at the airport, but he didn't reply. I was relieved, since that meant I didn't have to make up additional details and run the risk of being caught in a lie.

The Sheffields had reserved a place near Chamblee, so Rhys and I decided to hang out at Perimeter Mall until everyone made it into town. It wasn't close to the airport, but it was close enough to where they were staying that

I could come up with a plausible reason for being there if Dad pressed the issue. Besides, I wanted a hot pretzel.

"I don't like the idea of you staying in the house alone with him tonight," Rhys muttered. "There's no telling what kind of danger you might be putting yourself in, especially now that he's got two Cards."

I understood where he was coming from, but I still had a little bit of faith that the man who had largely raised me wouldn't bring me to harm without reason. "It'll be fine, Rhys. He's totally focused on this ritual, and as far as he knows, I'm bringing him two more batteries to power the spell. I really believe I'm his blind spot."

He shook his head, and it made me wonder if he was sensing something I couldn't—something in the Pattern that was sending him a warning. "That traveling god of yours have an opinion on this?" I prodded.

"Nah, nothing like that. At least I don't think so. Sometimes it's harder to see the Pattern clearly when emotions are involved. But Meili hasn't shown up or anything. If He had, I'd have told you."

I was certain he was playing it straight. "Alright, then. Don't be bothered about it. Dad needs me, at least for the next two days. Everything's fallen into place much better than he could have hoped a week ago. I'll be fine."

Rhys dipped a chunk of pretzel into his cup of yellow mustard and chewed grumpily. "Aria invited me to stay at their rental, but I'm staying in Priscilla so that I'll be nearby. Like I said, no deity advice, but my instincts say to stay close."

"Aw, you're worried enough to give up a flushing loo and a hot shower? I'm touched." I was trying to lighten the mood, but he scowled at me. "Really, Rhys, I'll be just fine. I'll keep my head down."

***

wo hours later and a check-in text with Dad later, I found myself
sitting in the living room of a rental house in the semi-posh heart
of Chamblee, a suburb of Atlanta which was only about fifteen minutes
from home. We were assembled in three distinct camps scattered across the
furniture. On the sofa and chair, Aria sprawled with her cousins Logan
and Paul. Lia, her mother Maddie, and Treigh sat stiffly on dining chairs
that had been pulled a few feet into the main room. Rhys and I stood near
the sliding glass doors which led out onto a lush green backyard.

"I know I've apologized to all of you," I began, "and I know that words
aren't enough to make you trust me, but I have to ask you for a leap of faith
here. After this is all over, if you want to tell me to sod off and never contact
you again, I'll respect that." The looks on all their faces left me unsure if
that's what would happen or not.

"Let's have a recap for the ordinary humans," Logan suggested, his voice
laced with sarcasm. "Why has Blair spent two decades on all of this?"

"Power and control," I replied simply. "He feels that our lineage was
shafted by the other Arcana back in the 16th century, that we were left
holding the bag while the other families fled to other parts of the world. He
feels that we were stripped of some of the social power we should have had
because our bloodline was nearly snuffed out after the failed Gunpowder
Plot."

"That's the Bonfire night thing," Treigh confirmed, and I nodded before
continuing.

"Right. Lots of people know about Guy Fawkes, but ..."

"Not in this country," Aria mumbled. "Most of us don't learn British
history in school."

"Yes, well, you lot have your own problems to focus on, I guess," I
acknowledged. "But anyway, those who *do* know about the Gunpowder
Plot often just write it off to Guy Fawkes since he was the one caught under
Parliament with enough gunpowder to blow King James to the moon. But
the real architect of the whole business was Robert Catesby, our ancestor

and the first Magician. He was pursued by the King's guards and then killed during a shootout. Fortunately, he had a son who had escaped with a relative before everything went pear-shaped."

I paused here to make sure everyone was keeping up, and it seemed that they were.

"Anyway, Robert's son—also named Robert—and his second cousin fled, taking the family history with them. They tried to find sanctuary with a few of the other Arcana families, but none let them stay longer than a night or two because they didn't want the King coming after them, too. Robert the Younger took that very personally, and thus began four centuries of generational trauma."

"That's a long time to hold a grudge," Paul Sheffield observed, rearranging himself in the overstuffed gray couch.

"Fair enough. But, as near as Rhys and I have been able to figure, Dad met Ellen at that music festival and they were drawn to each other but didn't know why."

"I suspect Mom sensed that he was special, but didn't realize he was Arcana. I've learned to recognize other Arcanas by their auras, but she wouldn't have known how to do that yet," Rhys interjected. "She hadn't been the Fool for very long, so she may not have understood what she was feeling."

"Anyway, Dad hadn't hatched his plan at that point, we don't think. But perhaps being skin-to-skin with another Arcana—even if he didn't know it—got his mental wheels turning and he cooked up the idea that if he had a litter of Arcana puppies, he might be able to start reuniting the Arcana under his leadership, the authority he felt our family had been denied all along."

"So then he used whatever research he had access to in order to start tracking down other Arcana families with fertile females? That's creepy and disturbing." Treigh rose and stood behind Lia, placing his hands protectively on her shoulders. She had toned down the war paint today, and opted for a H.I.M. tee shirt and black sweatpants with the moon phases depicted along the left leg.

"Creepy and disturbing, but not exactly world domination," Maddie offered. I wondered absently how offended she was at being a pawn in his seed-spreading game. "What could this ritual possibly accomplish?"

This is where my theories got murky, and Dad had been less-than-forth-coming about his original intent, so I had to forward my best guess. "I think that when he originally came up with the idea, the plan was to unite the Arcana into sort of a committee, with him at the head. Because he'd be guaranteed some loyal members—at least by his way of thinking—he'd basically be like the head of a shadow government, able to insert key people into positions around the world and influence policies. It would take years to insert people, but he wanted to set the foundation for a new age of the Arcana, with the Magician, or at the very least, his own descendents, in positions of power within the organization."

"I've met other Arcana who would have been sympathetic to that idea," Lia piped in. "The Tower tried to recruit me into a similar line of thinking when I first got my Card."

I nodded. "I don't know that he's had contact with them specifically, but I do believe he thought others would be in favor of unification. That was the idea he hinted at for most of my life, but since David's death, things have changed." My voice cracked as I pictured my brother's broken body, remembered wrapping it in a tarp.

Rhys laid his hand on my arm and continued. "When Blair inherited the Devil card, we have to assume that meant he was David's closest living relative, or at least the strongest one. It's not clear how Cards choose who to pass through when they aren't passed off intentionally, like mine and Zora's were. He now possesses the powers of both, and has two very dominant deities banging around in his skull. He may now be entertaining the idea that if his blood kin don't fall in line, he can simply take their power."

"By killing them?" Maddie was aghast.

I nodded. "Set is an evil god, already known for fratricide. I don't think Dad would jump to that idea on his own, but if Set were to prey on that four-century chip on his shoulder, mix in a little paranoia and delusions of grandeur ... Well, I don't think we can afford to assume he wouldn't go to that extreme. Maybe not straight murder, but putting us in great danger without concern for our safety because he would benefit by our deaths ... the point is that if this ritual succeeds, none of us will ever be safe."

"Doesn't that seem a little doomsday-ish?" Logan asked. "I mean, the guy is a douche—no offense—but killing his kids is a pretty big leap."

"I'd agree with you if I hadn't seen him escalate his violent behavior when he couldn't bring you lot on board willingly." I nodded to Aria and Lia. "I also saw how very quickly he pivoted to more scheming after David's death, and that was before Set showed up. Believe me when I tell you that there's no good end if he succeeds." I paused for a moment and let that sink in. I could feel my heart chakra throbbing, and vaguely wondered if anyone else could see it. "If there was any way to just avoid this, believe me, I'd be on-board. Even though I know how he manipulated me for most of my life, he's still my dad. I've grown up with him, been his sidekick and only confidante for most of my life. I don't *want* to go up against him. I'd rather just make a run for it. But ultimately, I have to listen to my own conscience and try to make amends for the wrong I've done."

"Making amends is good," Treigh began, "but that doesn't mean there's trust. You put Lia—and Aria—in danger."

"And Logan and his mom, too," I acknowledged. "I own that. But we're going to have to work together and have some level of trust to pull this off."

"For what it's worth, she's being honest." Aria's crown chakra gave off a soft glow. "She really is on our side right now." I couldn't blame her for adding the last two words.

"Alright, then." Rhys stepped forward and dialed his charisma up. "Zora and I learned a few tricks while we were in Florida. With my help, her chakra abilities can act as a conduit for our powers, allowing us to share them. We think that this is key to defeating Blair, but we need to prep Aria and Lia by clearing out and activating their chakras. This might take some time, so we need to get started."

"Then maybe tomorrow we can find a way to practice using our combined skills. I have to go home soon or Dad will be suspicious, and the day after tomorrow is when he plans to do the ritual."

***

O ne of the rooms in the rental had twin beds, and Aria stretched out on one while Lia took the other. I sat between them, closed my eyes and concentrated on opening each chakra in time with Rhys's reiki practice. Each time he cleared out one of their energy centers, the *pop* of connection came, linking them to the two of us.

When he was done, the girls sat on the edges of their beds and Rhys stood between the footboards of the beds. To my eyes, the room looked like a prismatic disco ball was on hyperspeed.

"This is so trippy," I commented.

"I can't see it, but I can sure feel it." Lia moved her hands through the brilliant bands of light. "It's like I'm electrified!"

Aria nodded agreement. "I don't know how my abilities would be useful in a sharing situation. I can call the Scales of Judgement, either to know if someone's lying or to force their karma into account. I don't really know what else I can do. Sometimes I can see ghosts, but that was true before I became Judgement. And so far, it's only been the ghosts of my ancestors on the estate where I live. Kind of a hyper-specific skill."

"We'll have to experiment with that," Rhys agreed.

"I can see ghosts, too." Lia was still playing with the electricity all around her. "I can also create glamours, affect the tides, and nudge people into doing what I want them to. Some of those might help. Probably not the tides one, though."

"I have the ability to see and read chakras, as well as increased physical strength if I concentrate on it. I'm not sure how that will jigsaw in either, but before I go, let's try a little experiment. Are you game?"

Everyone nodded.

"Right then. Close your eyes and picture what I describe to you. I'm going to try and push my vision of the chakra connections to you. Don't open your eyes until I say." They all obeyed. "Imagine that there is a deep red band of energy connecting all of us at the very base of our torsos, right where our legs meet. This energy grounds us. It is here that we are bound to our ancestors, and to each other, by blood."

"Energy harnessed and blood to blood," Lia intoned in a voice that wasn't quite hers. I looked at her closely, but the only thing that had changed was that the red bond between the four of us had intensified.

I pushed on. "Now imagine a fiery orange band of light connecting each of us. Its point of origin is just below your belly button." The orange trapezoid of light intensified. "A golden band connects each of us at our belly buttons, like umbilical cords. Through this bond, we can share our inner strength and personal power.

"Energy harnessed and blood to blood," mumbled Aria in that same haunted voice, like a radio from 100 years ago.

"From our hearts, a band of green light connects us. It is here that we'll find the ability to trust each other."

"Energy harnessed and blood to blood." Rhys this time, and when he spoke, the green band of light flared to a brilliant neon before returning to a more natural green.

"From our throats flows blue light, like pure water. May only honest words pass between us from now on."

"Energy harnessed and blood to blood." Whose voice was that? It took a moment for me to realize that it had been my own. Sort of.

"From our foreheads, we are bound by our third eyes in a deep indigo light so that we may see as the others see, and so we may see what the Universe wants to show us."

"Energy harnessed and blood to blood." We were now a discordant chorus of voices, though it seemed as though the words came from somewhere distant.

"And finally, a radiant violet band connects our crowns, our divine selves, as it hovers above our heads."

"Energy harnessed and blood to blood." When our involuntary voices finished this final chant, I could see the distinct outlines of each of my siblings' deities' auras behind them.

"Open your eyes." This was the test. Could I share my gift with them?

From the looks on their faces, the answer was a resounding *yes*.

Chapter 20

I rolled my suitcase up the front walk as darkness started creeping its way across the yard. It was a journey I'd made many times in the past three years since we'd first come to America. It had never really felt like home, yet I found myself hesitating as I stared at the house. How many more times would I cross this threshold? Even now, who would I find inside? Was there any trace of my Bàbá left?

A wave of emotion passed over me as I realized that the man I had known for most of my life might be gone forever. He'd been deeply flawed, as I'd found out recently, but he'd been the only constant thing in my life, and—until a little over a year ago—I had been the center of his world, and he'd been the center of mine.

I couldn't stop to dwell on that, though. The past weeks couldn't be undone. I focused on my solar plexus chakra and let my own personal power flow through me. It buoyed me, but my heart still ached. I took one brief moment to run my fingers across the rugged river rock that adorned the lower portion of the house's facade, then I took a deep breath and opened the door.

"Heya! I'm back!" I called. The house was quiet, but Dad's car had been in the garage, so I knew he was here somewhere. "Dad! Where are you?"

A faint rustling in the family room clued me in to his whereabouts. I passed through the foyer and into the open space which incorporated the family room and kitchen. Dad was sitting in an overstuffed armchair beside the cold fireplace.

"Oy! Dad, are you alright?" My concern was genuine and instinctive, and I quickly abandoned my suitcase and ran to his side. He was wearing the same outfit he'd been in when I'd left two days ago—had it only been that long?—and by the smell of him, he hadn't showered in that time either. His beard, usually neatly coiffed and scented with sandalwood, looked scraggly and wild. His pepper-and-salt hair was unkempt in what looked like bed head, but I'd wager he hadn't slept much, if at all.

"Dad, what's wrong?" He blinked but didn't reply. As much as I wanted to defeat his plan, I couldn't control the panic at seeing his condition. "Bàbá, please look at me!"

He blinked again, and this time, he slowly turned his head to face me. "Zora, my dearest," he croaked. "You've come home."

"Of course I've come home. What's happened here?" I looked around the house and nothing looked amiss, but something was off. "Dad, where are Tess and Darcy?"

"Oh ..." His expression was far away. "I had to shut them in the basement. Not to fret. I emptied their food bag down the stairs."

"What? Why?"

He held up his right arm, and I could see that the sleeve of his dress shirt was shredded and crusted with dried blood. "They didn't take very well to my new title, I suppose. Dogs can be frightfully territorial." His frame was wracked by a dry cough, and when it stopped, he sunk back into the cushion of the chair, exhausted.

"Bloody hell. I go away for two days and you completely fall apart." I used my usual saltiness to cover the fear I felt. "Hold on. I'm getting you some water and the first aid kit."

"Thank you, my girl."

I brought the water first, in a cup with a straw, and wedged it into his hand on the non-wounded side. Then I came back with moistened paper towels, scissors, and the first aid kit from under the sink. I knelt by the arm of his chair and cut away his sleeve at the elbow so I could work.

"You'll be lucky if this isn't already infected," I groused. "Now tell me what's going on while I patch you up."

He took a few tentative sips of water then closed his eyes like it was manna from heaven. "I'll try to explain. When you left, as you know, I had just activated the Devil Card. Well, it didn't take long for the deity to make Himself known."

I hesitated slightly in my Florence Nightingale routine. I wanted to mention that I had seen Set's outline, but I held back and focused on my work. Dad shifted slightly in his seat, and when I looked up, he had turned his eyes to me. His crown chakra pulsed with a weak lavender glow.

He studied me for a moment before continuing. "At any rate, Mercury was none too pleased about the new tenant. You are familiar with the Egyptian pantheon?" I nodded and he continued. "Well, the god Set presented himself, and he and Mercury ... disagree ... about how to co-exist."

I turned back to cleaning his arm with antiseptic and he sucked in air through his teeth at the pain. "I don't imagine they'd get on too well, given what each represents. Order and chaos are strange bedfellows."

"Just so," he agreed. "They've had a bit of difficulty coming to an arrangement."

"What does that mean?"

"Well, they are fighting for dominance, you might say."

I thought back on what I knew of the mythology. Mercury was a be-hind-the scenes player ... *the* player of the Roman pantheon. Set was always whinging about how his brother Osiris was the boss instead of Him. In fact, as I recall, Set did his brother in for it. Even chopped Osiris up into tiny pieces and scattered him all over Egypt, so the stories say. I imagine it'd be doing his head in to show up and find out there was already a horse in the stable. Plus, there ain't no love lost between the Romans and the Egyptians, historically speaking.

"So they're taking it out on you, then?"

"Not precisely. They're taking it out on each other, but since I'm the vessel, the row is taking place in my head."

"That explains why you haven't slept."

He nodded. "In fact, the first time they've stopped was when you walked in the door. Bless you for that."

"Yeah, well, I can't take credit. But you need to get some rest. You're proper clapped out." I finished bandaging his arm. "I'm going to wrap this in cling film and then you're going to take a shower and go to bed." It occurred to me that he couldn't cause much trouble if he was sleeping. Double win!

After doing his arm up like leftovers, I shuffled him off to the shower with instructions to burn his clothes afterwards because they smelled like death. He struggled to walk, but when I heard the water come on, I breathed a sigh of relief. I laid out his pajamas and then shot off a quick thumbs-up text to Rhys.

He wrote me back immediately.

Glad ur safe. Delete this text string. Gut feeling.

I thumbs-upped again and then did what he suggested. When the Fool has a gut feeling, you don't question it.

With that done, I thought it might be wise to check on the dogs. They'd never been particularly barky, so I wasn't surprised not to have heard much of a clamor from the basement, assuming they did, indeed, have food. I shut Dad's door so they couldn't cause him any more trouble.

As soon as I opened the door to the basement, I heard their claws on the tile and two pairs of eyes appeared at the bottom of the stairs.

"You look like Hellhounds," I scolded them gently as I noted the cascading trail of dog food down the stairs. And if they hadn't been let out in 24 hours, I was pretty sure there would be other messes to clean up, too.

Tess and Darcy seemed happy to see me, and were even happier when I opened the French doors to let them out. They were very well behaved and could be trusted to stay on the property, so I decided to let them do whatever business they needed to in the yard while I cleaned up whatever they hadn't been able to hold. I silently blessed whoever it was that had built this basement with a tile floor.

I swept up the mess of kibble as well, and retrieved their bowls from the kitchen, filling them with food and water. At the sound of sloshing in their dishes, the beasties chuffed and shoved their snouts in the water, lapping greedily. I sat on the downstairs sofa where David had spent so much time with his video games, and eventually the dogs came over and flopped around me.

They weren't vicious dogs, so I had to assume that one or both of them didn't like Set and saw Him as a threat. I recalled that they had acted a little strangely before I left for Florida, and assumed they must be sensitive to the change that had been happening within my father. I wasn't sure why, but it was comforting to know that the dogs rejected the new addition to the family.

After giving obligatory belly rubs, I found myself yawning mightily. I was a bit clapped out myself, to be honest, so I made sure the dogs were comfortable and then shut them back up in the basement. I would rather have kept them by my side, but that would be hard to explain, given that I knew they had bitten Dad.

I crawled upstairs, and it was no shock that I fell asleep shortly after I made sure Dad was off to Dreamland.

***

I woke the next morning feeling rested, but with a sense of unease. It was still early, just after eight ... too early to try and arrange for a meet-up with Aria and Lia to try and train with combined skills.

I headed downstairs and let the dogs out, then went back up to the kitchen for a cuppa and a bowl of cereal, clinging to the normalcy of the morning while it lasted. I was halfway through my second bowl of Apple Jacks when Dad cautiously cracked his door open.

"Safe to emerge?" he called out.

"Yeah, I tended to the dogs already. They're still in the basement."

"Ah, marvelous." Dad shuffled out in his pajamas, further evidence of how knackered he'd been. He never usually left his room until he'd showered and dressed. He plunked a pod into the coffee machine and hovered while it whirred out the magical wake-up juice. His back was still to me when he took his first sips and sighed in bliss.

When he turned to face me, I nearly choked on my artificially-flavored O's. It took me a moment to realize what was off about his appearance. His face was still familiar, but the features were now—how best to say this?—*asymmetrical*. The left side of his face looked much like the man I'd seen all my life, if a bit disheveled from going a couple of days without sleep. But the right side looked oddly more angular, as though someone had grabbed a pull-cord under his chin right-of-center and tugged it downward slightly. His right eye had a slightly sharper angle than the left, and his mouth dipped down just slightly, giving that side of his face the semblance of a permanent smirk.

"You doing alright?" I asked, wondering if he was aware of the changes in his face.

"I am," he answered slowly, almost languidly. "A good night's rest has done me a world of good." He sipped his coffee again and looked me in the eye, and I could see that even his eye color was slightly different. Both were still gray, but the right one had glints of green in it that I'd never seen before. "How about you update me on our *family* situation?"

It was a reasonable request, and one I expected, but the way he said *family* made my skin crawl just a little.

"Aria and Lia both made it in safely last night. Aria and her cousins are at a rental, and Lia and her mother and friend are at a hotel."

"They brought entourages?" he scowled, and the new proportions on the right side of his face made the expression even more menacing.

"I couldn't persuade them to come unaccompanied. Not surprising, all things considered. But Paul, Logan, Maddie, and Treigh have agreed not to interfere in the ritual.

He pondered this, and seemed somewhat mollified. "It's been awhile since I've seen Madelyn," he mused.

"I don't imagine it'll be a particularly fond reunion, if I'm honest," I commented, sipping my tea. "But they agreed to participating as long as it meant that we'd leave them alone going forward."

He turned so that I could only see his left side, the side that looked ... normal. He seemed lost in thought for a moment before he spoke. "That's my fault. I can see in retrospect that I've handled this all wrong. It would have failed entirely had it not been for you and your better sense. You cannot imagine how indebted I am to you for having the artfulness and diplomacy that I lack. Given the supernatural talents of the Magician, you would think I'd have been better at diplomacy, but I pursued an at-all-costs strategy, and failed utterly."

My jaw dropped open and I nearly dropped my cup. I'd never heard my father be contrite about anything.

He continued, "Zora, I realized last night that I have been a dictator to you for the last couple of years. A benevolent one, I'd like to think, but I still ordered you around and brooked no argument from you. Worse yet, and I hate to admit this, but I feel I owe it to you, I pushed your mind into complacency whenever I thought you might rebel against my wishes."

"I know," I said quietly, tears threatening to leak down my cheeks. Contrition *and* accountability? What was happening?

He nodded. "I should have known you would suspect it. It was inexcusable of me. And yet, last night, you were my savior. You swooped in and took care of me when I'd lost the ability to take care of myself. And even before that, despite my abhorrent behavior, you managed to convince the girls to come back. I know how hard that must have been after David ..." His voice cracked and my heart chakra exploded with energy. The tears that had been threatening to escape streamed down my cheeks. "Will you help me try to repair things with the girls? I've treated them like they were nothing but means to an end, but last night ... you called me Bàbá for the first time in forever, and it made me realize that they're my *daughters*, not my pawns. I need to make it right somehow once tomorrow night is over."

The last of my resolve crumbled and I leapt off my stool, abandoned what was left of my breakfast, and threw my arms around my father. I sobbed against his chest and he wrapped one arm around me, laying his cheek against my hair.

I couldn't think of what to say in reply. This wasn't the same man I'd been planning to betray, was he? How could I turn on someone who loved and trusted me so completely, who wanted to atone for what he had done?

Chapter 21

I stood in the shower, letting the scalding water run over my skin as if it could purify me. I hadn't set out to be a bad person, but now it felt like every decision I made—or might make—slid my karmic balance further into the red.

My father's heart-rending words played on a loop in my head, but so did the memory of carrying my dead brother to be sunk in the concrete foundation of some less-than-posh hotel. There was this tiny sliver of my heart that kept niggling at me, trying to convince me that my father could yet be saved. The worst part was how badly I wanted to believe it.

When the hot water ran out, I toweled off and squeezed my locs dry. Then I wiped my hand across the steamy mirror and stared at my own face, wondering who exactly would be looking back at me in two days' time.

Philosophical problems were too hard to tackle right now, so I decided to focus on a more pragmatic issue: how to make an excuse to see my siblings without arousing suspicion. My noodle was too cooked to be clever.

I pulled on an orange tank top and some camo pants, laced up my black work boots (which brought a reluctant smile to my face as I thought of

Lia's trademark Docs), and headed back downstairs, hoping some brilliant bit of dialogue would strike me when the moment came.

That same heart which had been shattering all morning leapt into my throat when I came down to find my father on the couch holding my cell phone.

"Aria texted you a few minutes ago," he said matter-of-factly. "She wants to know if they'll be seeing you today."

My pulse raced and I felt a shock of pain as adrenalin shot through me. "Oh, uh, yeah ... we had sort of talked about it, but didn't make a plan."

"That's nice that you're getting on so much better," he smiled, setting the phone down on the coffee table. I blessed Rhys for his Foolish hunch to delete his text string.

I stared at the device. Had he read all my texts back and forth with her? And the ones with Lia? Bloody hell, what had I said? Was there anything incriminating? Panic raced through me as I desperately tried to play it cool.

"I guess. She still doesn't like me, but I've been trying to make nice. Lia likes me even less."

He nodded, then looked up at me. I had forgotten how his face had gone slightly wrong, and it jarred me when I saw it again. "You seem hesitant to see her, though." That right eye twinkled just a little bit more than the left, and it was disconcerting.

"Dad, can I ask you a couple of very candid questions?" Every fiber in me wanted to put off the conversation, but in maybe thirty hours, the ritual would begin, and I didn't have time to spend sussing things out covertly.

He patted the cushion beside him in response, which put me on that dreaded right side. I recoiled on the inside but carried on.

"I want you to know how much I appreciate everything you said this morning," I began, and he half-smiled and patted my knee, encouraging me to continue. "There's something that's worrying me, though. You've always had uniting the Arcana as sort of your endgame, yeah?"

"Yes indeed. There's so much that could be accomplished over time. So much we could do to make the world a better place."

"And that's why you wanted to have Arcana kids, right? Because we'd sort of have a team to start with, and then we could try and persuade the other Arcana to join us?"

"Of course, Zora. I've told you all this before. What's your point?"

I swallowed hard, knowing the next two questions were pivotal. In the next thirty seconds, I'd know what I needed to do about the ritual *and* about my father. "Please know that I don't mean disrespect here ... I just want to make sure I understand ..." His brow furrowed, and the effect on the right side of his face made him look very much the part of the Devil. "You would mean to be the leader of this committee of sorts, am I right?"

He studied me for a minute before answering, and I could just feel his mind trying to slither into mine. I could also feel it running into what equated to mental mud—which surprised both of us, though neither reacted. It appeared that some of Rhys's immunity to persuasion had not yet completely faded from my *ajna*, my third eye. I was grateful for that, but I could tell that there were only the slightest tendrils left.

He responded with carefully-chosen words. "Certainly it would begin that way. I imagine the leadership seat would rotate eventually."

"Preferably to members of our family." It wasn't really a question, but I let him take it that way if he wanted to.

"Preferably, sure."

I was treading on dangerous ground, and I could see his crown chakra flickering while his illuminated third eye told me that he was trying to get a read on me. "I have to ask ... what would happen if members of our family didn't fall in line and agree with your point of view on whatever issue was on the table? Would you be satisfied to leave it to a democratic vote?"

His eyes narrowed somewhat, and the color of his right eye flashed with even more flecks of green. "I'm confident that we'd be in agreement, but your siblings are still children. When making large decisions, children shouldn't have the same say in business affairs as adults, should they?"

"Well, no, I suppose not. But I was thinking more of the future. Say five years from now."

"I would do my best to persuade them, but they'd be entitled to their opinions." His throat chakra flashed, telling me that he wasn't giving me the whole truth.

He still wasn't answering my question, though, and we both knew it. I had to push once more. "So you'd be cool with it at that point if you got outvoted, then?"

"What are you implying, Zora?" There was an edge to his voice now, and his crown chakra glowed the color of an aubergine. I didn't really have Spidey Senses like Rhys, but I knew I was dancing on a dangerous line.

"Not implying anything." I patted his hand soothingly. "I just wanted to know where things stood." It occurred to me only at that point that I'd been implying that Aria and Lia might not be willing to fall in line for him, and that might put them in danger.

He gripped my left hand tightly with his right. "I think that all of this has put a terrible strain on you, particularly since David's death." A violet aura with a familiar shape began to emerge along his right side, and I could just make out the shadowy canine-esque features of the Egyptian god. "You must be mentally exhausted, my dear." Dad's mind pushed at mine yet again, and with Set's strength behind it, I felt the last defensive effects of Rhys's power float away like feathers in a breeze. "So very tired, I can tell."

As he said it, I felt mental and physical fatigue wash over me. He was right; I *was* tired.

"You've been through so much, my girl." His voice felt like a warm duvet right from the dryer. "You deserve to rest a bit. Why don't you take a nap? I'll watch over you. I'll take care of you just like you took care of me."

Comfort flooded through me, and I felt safe and loved. What could it hurt to catch another hour or two of shut-eye? It was still early in the day. I had plenty of time ...

"I'll order some food and wake you when it gets here. Perhaps a nice big brunch, maybe an Eggs Benedict ... "

I love Eggs Benedict, I thought happily. *That sounds wonderful.* Just the notion of such a filling and delicious meal made my eyelids heavy.

"Maybe some pancakes and fruit, too ... " His voice was floating away from me and I was drifting on warm air currents. I couldn't even feel my body except for his strong hand holding mine. My muscles relaxed one by one and I sighed in contentment as I slipped into the dark.

***

The rest of the day passed in a haze. I'd half wake up, then doze back off, like I was under anesthesia or trying to get over the flu. I had a vague notion of something being amiss, of impending danger. But try as I might to hold onto consciousness, it slipped through my fingers like desert sand.

When my waking mind decided to stick around, the sun was high in the sky, sometime past mid-day. The rumbling in my gut, though, told me it wasn't the same day as it had been when I fell asleep.

I pried my eyes open and realized that I was inside what looked to be a large, empty warehouse. I also realized that my hands were handcuffed behind me, my arms wrapped around a steel girder. A bottle of water with a straw in it sat off to my right, and if I bent myself just so, I could reach it with my lips. I leaned over and sucked it dry like I'd spent a week in a desert. I was so thirsty that I didn't even care if the water was spiked.

One need satisfied, I surveyed my surroundings. Honestly, the place looked like a movie set where spies arranged clandestine meetings or mob bosses held hostages. The ceilings were maybe 25 feet high and held up by what looked like naked girders. The walls were mostly cement block, and there were large panels of windows on parallel sides. Some of the windows had been reinforced with boards, most likely sporting damage from some kids' target practice, while others were grimy and too high to see out of. Only a handful gave a view of the aquamarine sky.

I could see Dad's SUV parked on the far side of the empty room, and rustling noises told me that he was probably in the small office in the far corner. Every instinct told me to try to escape, but Dad had opted for handcuffs since he knew that duct tape, zip ties, and maybe even rope might not be enough to hold me if I tapped into my Arcana Strength. There was a chain a few inches long between the cuffs, so they weren't as uncomfortable as they could have been, but there was no pulling them apart. Highly specialized equipment, this. It was like kidnapping was his go-to negotiation method.

I closed my eyes again and visualized the island, reaching out to Shakti for help. She crossed the bridge in her demon-fighting aspect, weapons in each of her 10 hands.

"The time has come to fight," she said as she brandished a particularly nasty-looking serrated blade.

"Thanks for the heads-up, but my body is chained to a pole at the mo. I've been unconscious for about 24 hours, if I'm guessing right."

"The Magician's doing, no doubt," she hissed, and her skin took on a slightly blue tinge, her jet-black hair swirling in a wild mane behind her head .

"I suspect it's more the Devil's doing than the Magician's, if I'm honest. I ... don't know what to do."

"Get free."

"Cheers, that's very helpful. And what if I can get free? I have no idea where I am, but I'd lay odds that it's the location where the ritual is supposed to take place. Aria and Lia could be on their way here, and I have no way to warn them." Rage poked at my mind, and my heart chakra felt like broken glass.

Shakti lowered her weapons somewhat and regarded me. "He fooled you."

I thought back to the gentleness and kindness and affection he'd shown me the prior morning, and my chest felt like it was being crushed in a vise. "I don't understand it. He wasn't lying—I would have known. But then he mind-zonked me for a whole day and now I'm chained to a pole."

"He serves two masters now. The human mind, even one with Arcana blood, is not meant to hold that much divine energy. He may well be … damaged."

I considered this. "But Set can't make him do things that are against his nature, can He?"

She shook her head sadly. "No, he can only capitalize on tendencies that already exist. Set can bring out and amplify those."

How many times could my heart break in a span of two weeks? "So he was lying about how much I meant to him, even if my powers didn't pick it up."

"Oh, child, it would be so much easier for you if that were true. But he can mean those things and also give in to the darkness within him. It may be that he values you *more* when you do what he wants, but I think you know that there is a part of him that cares for you. You must remember this, Zora. Just because someone cares for you does not mean that they are good for you."

It was a hard lesson for someone who had led such a sheltered existence. But I didn't have time to wallow in self-pity. I had people who were counting on me for protection. "Any last bits of advice before I try to play superhero?"

"Just this: remember that you are Strength, and that Strength comes in many forms. You have explored some new avenues for that, and those are important. But also remember that BECAUSE you are Strength, the others will look to you for leadership. The ability to guide them and unify them is yours and yours alone."

"Rhys said something like that, too."

"The Fool's title is misleading. His innocence makes him wise."

"Thank you, Shakti. Will you stay close in case I need to call upon you?"

"I am always close, Zora. My strength and power is a skin you can wear anytime you wish. This construct," she waved at the island and the bridge, "is a device you created to help yourself focus. Focus faster." She winked at me, and the slightest smile tugged at my lips.

***

I opened my eyes, and time had clearly passed because Dad's SUV was gone. The sun was lower, but not yet setting, so I guessed it was sometime around 5 p.m.

Job one was to free myself from being shackled like a prisoner. Physical strength wasn't going to break handcuffs or chains, and I was hoping I could get loose without dislocating my thumbs. I'd seen that in movies, and I didn't relish the thought of that kind of self-inflicted pain. My mind started churning, and something about my position reminded me of one of those hand-held puzzles that required a lot of twisting and manipulation to untangle. I thought of my bound arms as a link in a chain, and the girder as an unbendable metal rod.

I started by pushing myself off the ground with my hands and scooted my back up the girder until I was standing. I tried shimmying my hands out of the cuffs until my wrists were slick with sweat and red from rubbing against the metal. I had to try and turn around so I could see what I was doing.

I dropped my wrists low and wriggled until I could get a leg backwards through the circle formed by my arms. Once one was through, the other wasn't as hard. I'd successfully turned around, but now my forearms were crossed and the cuffs were still on the other side of the beam. I tried pulling a wrist through now that I had a better angle, but the bindings were tight enough that my palms wouldn't fit. I REALLY didn't want to dislocate my thumbs to get out of this.

Maybe I could pull harder if there were something between the metal and my skin, a sort of protective layer. Dad hadn't bothered to gag me, so I didn't have a bandana or anything. I slid one of my shoes off, bent down, and hooked my sock with my thumb. I peeled it off and held it tightly. I only had one back-up if this didn't work.

It took several minutes, lots of swearing, and bending my wrists and fingers at unnatural angles, but I finally managed to thread the sock through the cuff, creating a barricade between the steel and skin. Then I bent over again and stood on the ends of the sock for leverage. I tried pulling my hand free again, and while there was some scraping on the back of my hand, I could put a lot more pressure on the wrist. Millimeter by millimeter, I slid my hand free.

I still had the cuffs dangling from my right wrist, but at least I wasn't chained to the beam anymore. I was free, or a reasonable facsimile thereof. But now what?

I checked my fitness tracker. 5:34. I gave myself a mental pat on the back for not being terrible at telling time by the position of the sun.

There was no telling where Dad had gone or when he'd be back, so I had to decide whether to try to escape the location or stick around. If I fled the scene, I'd have no way to warn the others about what had happened, and since Dad had already texted Aria (and possibly Lia?) once, I was pretty sure he'd done it again so that they wouldn't think I'd gone dark and get spooked.

That meant I had to stay. I did a sweep of the building, which didn't take long since it was really only three rooms. The warehouse space, the office, and a loo (which I was thrilled to have found, since I hadn't used one in a full day). The office held a large wooden desk and a few chairs which looked like they'd been purchased sometime in the mid 1970s, based on their avocado-green vinyl. I also saw that several of Dad's ritual supplies were collected in the office: candles, a small fire pit and wood, incense, five pounds of chalk powder, string, and a very nubby carpenter's pencil. Most of these seemed like pretty normal supplies for a ritual, so I moved on to check out the warehouse itself.

The building itself looked to be maybe sixty feet square, with bare concrete floors. In my search, I found the reason for the pencil being so worn down: Dad had used the string to draw a perfect circle with a diameter of about twenty feet, and then adorned it with a variety of sigils at key points. Some I recognized and some I didn't, and there were lines connecting them at all kinds of crazy angles. Something about the configuration was familiar, but I just couldn't place it.

My stomach rumbled, reminding me that I hadn't eaten in well over a day. I went and retrieved the water bottle, filled it in the sink and swigged it down. Not much I could do about hunger, but I could at least hydrate.

The windows were too high to see out of, so I decided to peek out the metal door which led to the outside. There were also three rolling garage doors, but there was no reason to mess with those. As I suspected, nothing outside the building looked familiar. Atlanta is a huge city, with a dozen incorporated suburban areas. I was in an industrial zone of some sort, and I had about zero chance of figuring out where I was without the GPS on my phone. A walk of the perimeter didn't give me any additional clues, but I hadn't expected any, so I wasn't surprised or disappointed.

I returned to the office and grabbed one of the tragically outdated chairs and, just to be sassy, pulled it over to where I'd been chained to the pole. Then I grabbed another to use as a footrest and plopped myself down to wait.

Chapter 22

It was another twenty minutes before the mechanized cranking of one of the garage doors heralded my father's arrival. Just enough time to spin me up sufficiently to throw a right wobbler if he so much as breathed on my temper's hair trigger.

He got out of the car and lowered the rolling door without so much as casting a glance in my direction. I bided my time, seething.

He finally swung his gaze my way and the start he gave at seeing my change in seating arrangements was satisfying enough to take a small edge off my anger.

"About time," I sneered at him.

It took him a minute to recover from the surprise, but more than that, the fact that I was free but still in the warehouse seemed to fundamentally confuse him. It took a beat, but he regained his composure and strode toward me. I could see that most of his face now carried that elongated quality that rather made him look like the Joker.

"I'm sorry I had to go to such lengths to keep you under control," he said amiably, and I ground my teeth.

"That was dirty pool," I spit. "What about all that rubbish about how much I meant to you and how much you appreciated me?"

His twisted smirk faded slightly. "It wasn't rubbish. I meant it, but I don't have time to be mucking about with your doubts and arguments at this stage."

"So you wouldn't have turned me into Sleeping Beauty if I'd asked you all this six months ago then?"

"I guess we'll never know." His voice was curt, impatient. "But I see that you're still here, and I assume it's not just to take the piss."

I was a little surprised at his use of slang. It wasn't something he did often. "In for a penny, in for a pound," I muttered. "Besides, I'm responsible for Aria and Lia coming here—assuming they still are. It'd be a pretty big etiquette error for me to dip out and leave them to your tender mercies."

"None of you will come to harm if you just quit giving me so much trouble. If you want to argue committee logistics tomorrow, fine. But I have work to do, and only about two hours to do it."

"By all means, don't let me stop you. But I'm starving, so I hope you at least brought some food."

He rolled his eyes and crossed his arms. It didn't seem like it to him, but I was playing my role very carefully. If I was submissive and forgiving, he'd know I was acting. But if I was too aggressive and confrontational, I might push him into another drastic action. He clearly didn't have a good handle on Set's influence, and it was making him unstable. I needed that to work to our advantage.

After staring me down for another thirty seconds, he stomped over to the vehicle and leaned inside. Then he stomped back and tossed me an apple. "This is all I've got at the moment," he grumbled. "Enjoy." Then he turned on his heel and strode into the office, returning with the bag of chalk.

"Are you going to help?" he snarled.

"I'm weak from hunger at the mo'," I replied, biting into the apple. "Check back with me in a few minutes. I'll just supervise for now."

His chest rumbled with what sounded like a growl, but didn't bother with a witty retort. Instead he walked over to the pencil-drawn circle and looked it over, maybe checking to make sure I hadn't messed with any of the symbols. Satisfied, he pulled out a small knife and punched a hole in the corner of the bag of chalk, pinching it shut to avoid accidental leakage.

I watched and chewed as he slowly let chalk powder out of the bag, tracing the large circle. He then started on the sigils, murmuring something that sounded a bit like Latin as he drew the powdered images over their pencil counterparts. When he was nearly done, I rose from the chair and stood near the circle, watching him finish.

Now that the sigils stood out in bright relief against the dark gray concrete of the floor, I recognized the picture in its totality. I didn't know a whole lot about Kabbalah or mysticism, but I recognized the diagram as the Tree of Life, and noted that some of the sigils resembled Roman numerals. I didn't know a bloody thing about the Tree of Life except that the lines within it represented some organized form of the Major Arcana.

"Nice work," I commented as he finished the last sigil.

"No thanks to you."

"Would you honestly have trusted me with drawing your precious symbols?"

He thought for a moment, then said, "Probably not."

"Alright, then," I said with an air of finality. It was an intricate dance ... letting him know that I was free to defy him, yet under his control at the same time. It kept him guessing, which was what I needed to do.

"Don't. Touch. Anything," he instructed, crumpling the now-empty chalk bag.

"Wouldn't dream of it. Are the girls still coming?" There was a mild panic in my heart, and I was hoping it wouldn't translate into my voice.

He smirked. "Of course they are. It's actually quite fortunate for me that your generation eschews phone calls for texting. I've chatted with them extensively, through *your* phone of course."

"Of course." My heart pounded, and I wondered what he might have learned from them. I prayed that they hadn't mentioned Rhys.

"They'll be arriving within the hour. I'll need you to return those chairs to the office. Their extra guests will need to wait in there while we take care of business out here."

I gave him a flat look but didn't argue. Instead I grabbed the top of each chair and dragged them back to the office, making sure that the ensuing racket was full-on annoying. I hated acting like a petulant brat, but it was all part of the show. I felt like David would be proud, and I wondered if his spirit was still with me, watching me behave the same way I'd counseled him not to.

When I stepped back out of the office, Dad was proper seething, but he bit his tongue and didn't say anything. I was poking the bear, and he knew it.

"I suppose you have cause to be angry with me." *That* was his olive branch? Weak at best.

"Thank you for acknowledging that being unjustly and magically sedated without my consent is a justifiable reason to be angry."

He set his jaw, but couldn't deny the logic of my statement. "Fair enough. I panicked. I couldn't have you deciding to have an attack of conscience when I'd been preparing for this for 20 years."

I held up the wrist that still sported the handcuffs. "I don't even want to know why you had these."

He didn't try to explain, and I was glad for that. "Look, I'll make it up to you. I was so exhausted from the two days of sleep deprivation, and I wasn't reasoning clearly. As I said, I panicked." And then as an afterthought, "I apologize."

I put my hands on my hips, but didn't offer any more smart remarks. I knew better. One aspect of him (maybe the Mercury part) was capable of being rational, but the other part (the Set part) was the essence of Chaos. If yesterday had taught me anything, it was that which aspect controlled my father could change in the blink of an eye.

"Be a dear and get the candles for me, will you?"

I didn't speak, but ducked back into the office and emerged with the box containing a dozen pillar candles. I had expected him to place them around the outside of the circle, but instead, he positioned them near the sigils representing points on the Tree of Life: three candles in a line on the left, four in a line in the middle, and three in a line on the right. There were two left over, which he positioned at the north and south ends of the outside of the circle.

I watched him assemble the small fire pit that he'd bought from some big box store. He loaded it up with kindling and small logs and then we carried it into the circle and placed it just north of center, between two of the candles. Then he shooed me out of the circle while he triple-checked to make sure that none of the sigils had been damaged by all our movement.

Finally satisfied, he took a deep breath and went to sit in the office. Against my better judgement, I followed him.

I plopped into one of the chairs and kicked my feet up onto the desk. Dad looked at me disapprovingly, but seemed to decide it wasn't worth making an issue.

"Do you want me to take the handcuffs off your wrist?" he asked, eyeing the shackles as if they were a bad fashion choice.

"No, I think I'll keep them on to remind me who I'm dealing with." The second the words left my mouth, I knew they were a step too far. I laughed to try to soften the remark, but to no avail. Dad's face contorted in anger for a nanosecond before he got control again. Or so I thought.

With alarming speed, he leapt up and swept my feet off the desk, almost causing me to go pitching out of the chair. "You have no *idea* who you're dealing with. But I'll tell you this, *my girl*," the moniker he used to say with affection was laced with acid. "If I can make you sleep for twenty-six hours, what do you think I can do to the minds of someone weaker in their powers than you are? Did Aria tell you what I can make people do?"

I shook my head, unsuccessful at keeping the fear out of my eyes.

"I made a random man at a nearby table stab himself in the leg with a salad fork. I could have made him stab himself in the jugular, had I been so inclined. What do you suppose I could do to the guests who will be occupying this office during the ritual?"

He narrowed his predatory eyes at me, and I shivered. He didn't need to give me a mind push to paint a picture of the carnage he could cause if we didn't behave.

"Ah, you understand now, don't you? So don't get any cute ideas about mucking up the ritual. Now, if I were you, I'd get comfortable until the rest of the *family* gets here and give over trying to annoy me. You are on less steady ground that you realize, and you will *not* spoil my plans." He pointed a finger at me and stepped forward. I was too afraid to move, and besides, there was nowhere to go. I gritted my teeth and tried to wear a bored expression, but I didn't think it worked too well.

When his finger was less than an inch from my face, his crown chakra erupted into a purple blaze, and I fell into a vision, a gift from Set, no doubt. The fact that I knew it was a vision did nothing to mitigate the horror.

The same office, but the daylight had faded into night. There were four bodies in the room. Maddie Alvarez lay sprawled across the desk, her mouth agape and her neck purpled with bruises. Paul Sheffield lay in a heap in the corner, his neck also bruised, but the deep divots in the drywall above him indicated that choking alone hadn't been enough. Treigh's and Logan's forms were crumpled to the ground, the centerpoints of elaborate blood splatter. Both of their bodies were face-down, but each held sharp pieces of metal in their lifeless hands.

My own scream ripped me out of the vision and my stomach heaved, expelling the apple I'd eaten with such attitude earlier, as well as most of the bottle of water, into the trash can beside the desk.

"Now dispose of that somehow and then sit like a good girl," a voice that wasn't quite my father's hissed. "Our guests will be arriving soon."

Chapter 23

Fear of the unknown might be one of the only constants in the Universe. I felt pretty chuffed when all my sibs agreed to band together. I felt cautiously optimistic when I realized that we could bind our powers together with a little effort.

But all of that counted for naught when I had no way of knowing what had happened for the last day. Worse yet, I had no idea what *they* thought happened.

That made me think that, in retrospect, our plan had been flimsier than we'd imagined. One weak link and the whole chain might be broken beyond repair.

My hopes weren't buoyed when I heard the other cars pull up outside the rolling door, which my father had conveniently closed behind his own vehicle. Couldn't have randos walking by and seeing an elaborate metaphysical ritual, after all.

I moved to open the door, but one venomous look from the Arkhamed-out version of my father's face told me I wouldn't be getting anywhere near enough to our guests for a private conversation. The knot in my gut twisted again, threatening to weaken me with more heaving, even though there was nothing left in my gut. I took deep breaths and tried to center, focusing on calming the tides in my solar plexus chakra, the seat of personal power. I felt a slight tingle from my crown—Shakti telling me She was with me—and my stomach settled a bit.

"Well, well," my father began with thickly-applied charisma. "Madelyn. You look as lovely as I remember."

"Can it, Dorian. You put my daughter—and don't you dare say *our* daughter—at risk, and I'm only here to make sure that doesn't happen again. I only consented to this because I was *assured* that you would leave her alone going forward." Maddie brushed past Dorian, her eyes scanning the room. When she spotted me, she released a slight sigh of relief.

Treigh followed, positioning Lia squarely behind him. "You're going to need to step back, *sir*," he said in mock courtesy. "Lia requires that you respect her personal space."

Though I was seeing him from the side, my father's smirk was unmistakable. "And you're here to insure that, are you?"

"I am," Treigh answered with the confidence of someone quite used to kicking arse if necessary. He didn't know what I knew, and the bloody vision I'd seen of Lia's best friend made me shiver. He didn't know that his physical strength was no match for what Dad could do to his mind.

"How lovely that she has someone to protect her." The tone was unmistakably sarcastic, and Dad made a show of stepping back with a deep bow. Treigh's eyes narrowed, and he escorted Lia to stand by her mother. His intimidating glare would have made the Secret Service proud.

Once they were in, Paul's lean figure came into view. He didn't say anything at all, but his expression of hatred was evident as he stalked past my father.

Aria came next, and her face was almost as frightening as Dad's. So much so that he took a step back involuntarily. I smiled and reminded myself—if we lived through tonight—to ask her what she did to him last month. Her eyes swung to me, and I saw her register the cuffs that still dangled from my left wrist. Her brow furrowed for an instant as she met my gaze, and I nodded ever-so-slightly to indicate that I was okay.

Finally, Logan's large silhouette filled the doorway and he stopped just inside, crossing his arms across his chest. Under different circumstances, Logan and Treigh would have been a very powerful pair of enforcers.

I noticed that the door didn't *click* when he shut it, and my heart crossed its fingers that that was a good sign.

"Now that we're all here, why don't we all make ourselves comfortable?" Dad ushered everyone toward the office. I had tossed the trash can into a dumpster outside, and I desperately hoped that the office didn't reek of my sickness. "Why don't the four of you," he indicated the non-Arcana members of the bunch, "have a seat while we're going about our business?" I saw his crown chakra flare, and Maddie, Paul, Logan, and Treigh took seats on the chairs.

For all intents and purposes, it looked like they were just agreeing to his request, but my Sight told me that wasn't the case. They were under his influence already, and I cringed. Dad took a breath, and his throat chakra sprang to life.

"Marvelous. Now, let me begin by saying that I deeply appreciate you making the journey here, even though the methods by which I originally tried to persuade you were ... questionable. I am thankful to Zora for persuading you to come. I'll try not to take too much of your time."

"Good," Lia replied curtly. "The faster I can get out of here and head home, the better." Her candor told me that she wasn't falling under his normal influence, and that was reassuring. But if Set decided to put the whammy on her, it might go differently.

"Let's step out to the ritual circle, shall we?" Dad gestured toward the door, indicating that I should lead the group out. I had no doubt that he was making sure I never got a chance to utter so much as one private word to Aria or Lia. I wondered if the girls even noticed that their four supporters didn't so much as bat an eye as we walked out of the room.

Though we'd only been in the office for a few minutes, unfamiliar magic prickled along my skin as we re-emerged into the main warehouse. The fading sunlight streamed through the panels of windows, and the dusky blue evening sky peeked through the dusty skylights. I ran my hands up my bare arms at the sensation, and I caught Lia shuddering as well.

"You can feel the alignment, can't you?" Dad asked, his eyes flashing. "We're only a few minutes away. It will create a perfect conduit for our work here tonight."

I don't think I'd considered too much what the alignment might mean for our individual powers, but the auras and chakras on each member of our family glowed just a little bit brighter than normal to my Arcana eyes. I wasn't sure if that was because the heavenly bodies were juicing my Sight up, or if it was because all of our powers were supercharged. There was no way to tell, since I had nothing to compare it to. We stepped over to the area where the elaborate chalk drawings covered the floor.

"What's all this?" Aria asked.

"It's rather complicated to explain, and I'm not sure we have the time for an in-depth lesson, but let me see if I can condense it to what you need to know." His throat chakra was pulsing, and I could see the energy reaching out toward my sisters. His magic would be bolstered by the alignment, too, and that added another layer of frosting onto my anxiety cake.

I caught my breath when I saw the golden tendrils get repelled by silvery-white aura force fields that flashed when his influence tried to get through. *Rhys*, I thought to myself, and almost wept with relief. His natural resistance was still pulsing through their energy fields, but I wasn't able to tell if our father felt the magical ricochet. As Dad began his explanation of the Tree of Life, I hazarded a glance over to the warehouse door and saw that it was now completely closed. I hoped that meant Rhys had made it in here somehow.

"The Major Arcana and the Tree of Life, which is the shape you see here, are intertwined in many ways," my father explained. "It's also known as the

Kabbalah, and represents the thirty-two paths to wisdom. The ten points are known as *spheres* and represent the different powers of the Divine Being. The lines between the spheres represent the twenty-two Major Arcana Cards, each of which represents its own divine characteristics. That's highly simplified, and I've omitted the theology and philosophy from it, but you get the point. I'm recreating—as near as I can guess—the ritual that was used to make the Cards in the first place. I've made a few tweaks to unite the Arcana rather than dividing them."

"So what are we supposed to do?" Lia, who had spared no expense in her glam goth war paint tonight, took a step toward the circle. She was clenching and unclenching her fists, either because the moon was part of the alignment and sending power zinging through her or because she was as nervous as I was.

"Nothing yet, my dear." Dad stepped ahead of her to prevent her from entering the circle prematurely. "When the time comes, all you have to do is stand on the line which corresponds to the Moon. Aria will stand on the Judgement line, and Zora will stand on Strength's line."

"And you'll stand in the Magician's place?" It was the first time I'd spoken, and it was a pointed question, but he had no reason to think that the others knew anything about David at all. As far as *he* knew, they weren't aware he was also the Devil.

"Well, naturally," he smiled, and it was clear that my jab didn't go unnoticed. He inclined his head slightly toward the office, and the meaning wasn't lost on me.

I closed my eyes, trying to balance, and concentrated on keeping a flow of energy through my chakras. I reached my mind toward Shakti for help and felt the warmth of Her presence. When I opened my eyes again, I felt calmer, but still had no idea what to do to keep my sisters safe.

Dad directed Aria to take a position on the bottom left, just outside the circle, and pointed for Lia to mirror her position on the right. Then he moved clockwise around the circle until he was standing just past nine o'clock. "Zora, you'll start your position here. The line going all the way across here is yours." That put me on the far side of the circle from his SUV, and also meant that if I had to dive or dodge, I had nowhere to duck and cover. Lia might be able to make it behind the vehicle if things went wonky, but Aria and I were too far away to get there quickly.

"I'll be here." He pointed at a line on the top left of the diagram. As he passed me, I felt a chill which raised gooseflesh up my arms, despite the summer heat. You're all to hold your positions outside the circle until I tell you to move into position. Is that understood?"

"Just to verify," Aria spoke up, "after this is over, I can go home, and that's the end of it, right?"

"If that's what you wish," he shrugged. "Once the ritual begins, you need only to hold your position until it's over. If anyone exits the circle prematurely, the magical backlash would likely strip them of their powers, and quite possibly cause serious injury." His chakras remained steady, telling me that was no bluff.

We all nodded, and my mind scrambled to come up with a plan on the fly.

"There is one more thing." He pulled an ornate knife the size of his index finger out of his shirt pocket. "I must have a drop of each of your blood. You all know, I assume, that the Cards are forged by blood magic.

"That doesn't seem like it's sanitary," Lia remarked.

"I'm afraid we'll have to risk it," our father smirked. "I'm right out of alcohol wipes." He started with me, of course, figuring that I was under enough of a threat that I wouldn't try anything. He was right. I held out my index finger and the dangling handcuffs glinted in the fading sunlight. Then he pricked me just hard enough to make a large drop of blood slide down the shiny silver blade. Being very careful to keep the blade flat so the blood co-mingled, he repeated the process with Aria and Lia, then himself.

He picked up the candle at the top of the circle and held the blade in its fire, then walked around the circle, lighting the candles one by one and warming the blade in each flame. We were close to beginning the ritual, and I had no clear plan. I hated doing things without a plan.

The best thing I could think to do was to try to enact the sliver of a plan we'd come up with two days ago. I centered myself and focused each of my chakras in turn until I felt completely in balance. Then I remembered what I had learned from Ellen and Rhys about energy, and visualized those glorious rainbow colors reaching out to each of them.

When I opened my eyes, I could see the glow of the colors around me, but they didn't seem to be taking root in Aria and Lia. My heart pounded hard in my chest as doubt flooded over me. Was the extra power from the alignment somehow messing with my ability to direct the fingers of light?

"Now," my father ordered, "on the count of three, you will each step to the location I showed you. You must step OVER the circle, and the tips of your toes should be touching the line that corresponds to your Card, but you must NOT—and I can't emphasize this strongly enough—damage the design or the sigils." He looked at each of us to make sure we understood. "Alright, one ... two ... three."

We moved like a choreographed dance, Dad included, and stood where we were told. The surplus energy had me buzzing before, but stepping onto the line on the Tree of Life sent a jolt through me that felt like lightning. Dad reached again for the candle at the very top of the circle and held the blade over it as he had at the beginning. "Energy harnessed and blood to blood," he intoned, and Aria's and Lia's eyes opened wide, hearing him echo the words that they themselves had channeled two days ago.

There was a flare of light from the candle, and the glow dripped down like magma onto the tip of the chalk line on which Dad was standing. The light flared along his line, like a fuse that stayed lit, and when it reached the next sphere, it split into three, traveling along the other Arcana lines in the diagram. I felt a tingle in my toes as the light traveled along the Strength line, and when I tried to shift my weight, I was alarmed to discover that my feet were now rooted to the spot.

I was so busy staring at the golden lines that a gasp escaped my lips when I spotted a pair of feet I hadn't expected toeing the line immediately opposite my father. Dad was surprised, too, but instead of a gasp, a deep bellow erupted from his throat.

There, on the line belonging to the Fool, stood Rhys, hands crossed over his chest, and eyes dancing with amusement at our father's rage.

"Hey. I'm Rhys. My mother sends her regards."

As if Rhys were a magnet, the brilliant tendrils of color (which had been waving out of my chakras like one of those crazy inflatables at a car dealership) snapped into place, connecting me, Rhys, Lia, and Aria. A grin spread across all our faces as we felt the bond and our eyes all blazed a silvery gray. Dad couldn't see the lights, but he could see our smirks and our eyes.

He looked at me with crazed eyes. "I warned you," he hissed.

From inside the office, Madelyn Alvarez's scream ripped the air.

Chapter 24

"He's going to make them hurt each other!" I screamed.

"Not if he wants this ritual to happen, he isn't," Rhys replied. "I have no problem turning his mind inside out, and then where will his little plan be?"

I stared at Rhys. What the bloody hell was he talking about? That wasn't one of Rhys's powers. The flicker in my brother's throat chakra told me it was a ruse, and I tensed, worried our father would see through it. Dad fixed his gaze on his oldest son ... the one he hadn't even known existed. He looked both enraged and confused.

We heard a crash from the office, but no more screams. I hoped that didn't mean it was too late for Maddie.

I felt Rhys tug on the golden solar plexus tether and the eggshell-like protection I'd seen him use before enveloped the four of us, reinforcing that even if Dad's power increased dramatically when the alignment was complete, he wouldn't be able to control our minds. But that protection didn't extend to the people in the office, and I feared the worst.

"How *dare* you interfere with this ritual?" I could see my father's crown chakra sparking, and my guess was that Set and Mercury were arguing about which one of them was going to take control of this situation.

"How dare *you* threaten your own children and their loved ones just to get your way?" Lia chimed in. The purple glitter in her eye makeup shimmered in the setting sunlight, a stark contrast to the double-winged black eyeliner that made her look like a dragon ready to devour some foolish mortal.

"I had no intention of harming any of you. You all agreed to come here." His throat chakra flickered.

"He's lying," I told my siblings. "He definitely meant us harm." My greatest fear was laid bare. Whether physically or magically, my father had every intention of this ending badly for his children.

"Is that so?" Aria lifted her hands, palms up, and her crown chakra sprung to life.

Fear flashed in Dad's eyes, and I had an inkling of what had frightened him before. I'd seen her make that gesture at me, and it shook me to my core. I knew now that she was calling forth the Scales of Judgement, and with her Goddess Ma'at working through her, that might mean some really bad juju for Dad.

Lia held her arms out and tugged on the green heart tether. "You do have a lot to answer for," she smiled, and it sure looked to me like this dragon was about to breathe fire. My father's face went pale and he cast an agonized glance behind me.

"That wasn't my fault! I didn't do anything to him!"

I swiveled my head around to look at the line where the Devil was meant to stand. I didn't see anything, but I had no gift for seeing ghosts. Then again, Lia also had a talent for illusion, so there might be nothing there to see.

Something that felt like an earthquake hit all of us simultaneously, and the corresponding lightning through my veins told me that the alignment had officially begun.

Dad's crown chakra blazed in violet fury, and the outline of the beast-headed god emerged, creating a deep aura a foot outside my father's skin. Dad's eyes flashed, and a tick later, I was seeing stars. The pain arcing through my brain was agonizing, and from the howls around me, my siblings were feeling it, too, even Rhys. We were all gripping our heads as if we were trying to keep our brains from tearing their way out.

But Rhys's wasn't the only male voice I heard wailing ... I forced my vision to focus on my father, and he was clutching his head as well. The form of Set pulsated as another spectral form emerged from my Dad's crown chakra. The shadow of Set grew smaller as the image of Mercury grew.

The battle within my father was disruptive enough to lessen the clawing pain in my dome, and I tried to think of how to exploit this break in the agony. An idea occurred to me. "You can't have the Devil occupy the Magician's place on the Tree," I yelled. "Didn't think of that, did you?" What was left of Set's shape turned directly toward me and, though He made no sound, his great maw opened.

If I thought I'd known pain before, I was sorely mistaken. White-hot energy seared through me like lava on my brain, and I screamed in a chorus with my siblings. I was losing my grip on the tethers, so I focused hard on the deep red light of the root chakra, anchoring myself to the essence of who I was, and pushing that strength out to my brother and sisters. Even if my brain melted, maybe they could still find a way through.

My vision began to clear, and though the pain wasn't significantly lessened, I found that the more I focused on the root chakra, the more I was able to maintain energy flow to all the others. I hazarded a glance at them, and it appeared that they were no longer suffering from the blinding headache. That was good for them, anyway. I, however, felt like I was being shredded from the inside with a hand-blender.

I remembered what Ellen said … I was like a battery, and I made all of their powers stronger. I watched as Aria raised her hands again, Ma'at standing tall behind her.

"You have done horrible things, Dorian Blair," came a voice that was a mix of a 16-year-old and an immortal being. "You have caused pain, suffering, and death. You have bastardized the miracle of giving life for your own selfish purposes. You have manipulated, lied, and committed abuse. You must be judged."

My father raised his arms and the figure of Mercury, which now reigned supreme in Dad's aura, raised his as well. The perimeter of the circle erupted into a fiery glow, and the sigils reflected the light like blazing mirrors. "YOU WILL NOT KEEP ME FROM WHAT IS RIGHTFUL-LY MINE! YOUR BLOOD AND YOUR POWERS ARE MINE TO CLAIM!"

I trembled as I tried to pour strength into Rhys, Aria, and Lia. The pain was tearing me apart, and I could see the flesh on my arms beginning to shrivel as I forced Strength through the arteries of energy that bound us. Only the brush of Shakti's spirit kept me from collapsing.

This is your power, she whispered in my mind. *You are the font of Strength. Your faith pushes them past what they think they can endure. You are the light that binds them.*

I felt a push to my throat chakra coming from Rhys and a vision of the Pattern danced before my eyes: a vision of blood flowing out of my father and into each of us. At first, I was seized with terror, but Rhys's clarity flowed through the bond, and suddenly I realized what I was seeing.

"WRONG!" I bellowed, and though the mouth was mine, the Strength in the voice was Shakti's. "You have it backwards. The power is OURS, because not only do we have our own blood, our own magic, we have yours, too!"

Lia's voice rang out, with a musical quality that was all Selene. "The Magician in our blood gives us wisdom, power, and authority. You cannot take our power away, though some of it may have come from you."

"And now the Scales must be balanced," Aria intoned. And then in a voice that was most definitely not hers, she said, "Today is not your day, Cousin."

Set's form roared forth as Ma'at's words floated in the air, and Aria's hands were stretched out in front of her, palms up, but at different heights. Her face was clearly strained as she forced her hands level with each other, and the energy she pulled from my solar plexus tether felt like sternum cracking outward. My voice was raw with the agony of my shrieks, but I couldn't hear myself over the wail that erupted from my father.

Lia extended her arms skyward, reaching for the moon, and Selene's silvery form shimmered around her. Gravity pressed down on us, and the golden light that had marked the circle and the Tree paled to match the Moon's luminescence. The heaviness threatened to snap my bones, and my ebony skin paled to a dull gray.

Rhys had remained silent throughout the proceedings, and I peeled my aching eyes away from my father to see what had become of my remaining brother. His eyes were closed and fluttering, and pulsating tendrils of his pale blue power reached out to Lia, and her blazing eyes fixed on the form of Set.

She opened her mouth, and I watched in terror as a spectral hand reached out of her mouth and extended across the circle. I had expected the hand to grab Set, but instead it stopped halfway across the circle, hovering between Aria and me. A hazy mist formed on the line underneath it and climbed upward through the heavy air toward the ghostly arm. The hand turned its palm up, as if in offering, and as the mist flowed into it, the haze began to take shape: the ephemeral shape of a lanky teenager in a hoodie.

David. I could feel tears sliding down my cheeks, though my raw voice had screamed itself out. I felt my life force waning, and I was glad that I'd gotten to see him before joining him on the Other Side.

Lia closed her mouth and the arm she'd extended disappeared, but David's translucent form remained. A movement from Rhys's direction drew my attention, and his eyes, now the electric blue of the sky, were fixated on me. His heart chakra flared a neon green and a burst shot through our tether like a bolt.

I gasped as the energy hit me. Had my feet not been magicked to the ground, it would have knocked me over with its intensity. The pain wracking my body didn't abate, but my skin's hue changed from the gray of ash to the brown of rich earth.

Aria's Scales glowed fiercely. "You have been Judged unworthy," she boomed. "You may choose Atonement or Reckoning."

Chapter 25

Dad sputtered incoherently in rage, and the creepy stretching of his face that had begun earlier intensified, bringing yet another Batman villain to mind. The schism trickled into his aura as well, until two separate divine outlines morphed and battled for dominance, creating a terrifying funhouse effect in his energy.

"The choice has been made." Ma'at/Aria's voice intoned.

"Let the Pattern be repaired." The deep and resonant echo came from within Rhys, and his own crown chakra flared to life. Though his feet were rooted like the rest of ours, he bent his knees into a deep squat. Then he raised his hands and slammed them down on the glowing chalk lines. The silvery lunar light exploded into a brilliant and icy blue, and when Rhys stood, the hulking outline of Meili stood behind him.

A chill and swirling wind began to blow within the circle, blowing out the candles and sucking up the chalk into its vortex. The glowing dust gave the illusion of a tornado of glittering ice, and the temperature dropped to match. Gravity slipped away as we were swept up as well, and the garbled shrieks of our father rose above the wind.

"Energy harnessed and blood to blood!" Rhys yelled above the din.

The now-familiar words echoed in my head, and I repeated them. "Energy harnessed and blood to blood!"

Lia's voice came next. "Energy harnessed and blood to blood!"

Then Aria. "Energy harnessed and blood to blood!"

And finally, a distant whisper which was somehow audible above the gale: "Energy harnessed and blood to blood!" David.

"Energy harnessed and blood to blood!" The divine spirits within my siblings and me shouted the words as our bodies spun in the icy Nordic air. Through it all, Dad was screaming, and my heart wept as images of the perfect Christmas in Lewes so many years ago tugged at my memory. I tried to push the thoughts away as I watched this twisted version of my father get sucked into the center of the whirlwind.

The rest of us continued to swirl around him, creating a perfect circle with Dad as the central point. Suddenly, the wind died, and we all hovered in place, the sparkling chalk sprinkling down on us like a diamond snowfall. The rainbow of chakra tethers snapped into place, creating a perfect circle of prismatic light anchored at five points.

Five.

David was connected.

The light flowed through his translucent chakras, but he was part of the circle just like we were. *Wicked,* came the feathery whisper from his translucent lips. I couldn't help but smile despite my physical and emotional agony.

The rainbow of light grew in intensity, one color bleeding into the other. The brightness became blinding white light, as though being refracted backwards through cut glass. I closed my eyes against it.

There was a loud *pop* and gravity returned, and though it hadn't been more than a few feet, my body crumpled to the ground like a rag doll. I lay still, just trying to breathe.

"Everybody okay?" Rhys's voice sounded far away. A series of mumbles answered him.

I pushed myself up to a seated position slowly, and my muscles deeply protested at any attempt to move. I peeled my eyes open to find us all in similar positions, shaky, and covered in a layer of chalk. Lia struggled to stand, Aria flopped on her back in a *poof* of white dust, and Rhys crossed his legs, looking us all over to make sure we were alive.

David's ghost was gone, and I missed him all over again.

Dad remained sprawled and unmoving in the center and a gnawing feeling clawed my gut.

With my limbs trembling, I began crawling toward him. I had to know the extent of what we'd done. We'd had no choice, but still ...

The others made no move, but watched me in silence. My heart thundered in my chest as I reached out to grab his shoulder and roll him onto his back.

His eyes were closed, and in this moment, it was almost like seeing him asleep. Despite the thin coat of chalk, the face that I looked upon was the familiar one I'd seen my whole life, all traces of the divine battle extinguished. I didn't have the strength to gather him to me, so I laid my forehead on his chest and wept hot tears.

"I knew you missed me," a voice rumbled from beneath my head.

I jerked my head up so fast, I nearly gave myself whiplash. His eyes were closed, but there was an uncharacteristic smile on his face.

"I ... I ... " I stammered, but no words came out. Behind me, I heard Lia and Aria running for the door to the office and whip it open. So many things happening at once! The vision of carnage Dad had shoved into my mind flashed across my memory, and I turned my head toward the small room, bracing myself for the agonized sounds I half-expected to hear. When none came, a band of tension loosened in my ribs.

Satisfied that there hadn't been a mass murder, I turned back to see my father struggling to sit up. A tiny trickle of blood dribbled out of his nose, and he swiped at it with the back of his hand. "Ouch. When did that happen?"

A blink later, I felt Rhys at my side. "Zora, are you okay?"

I leaned back against his leg. "All parts still attached," I croaked, "but I'm pretty sure I got hit by a meteor."

"Such a drama queen," my father quipped, examining the blood smear that extended from the back of his middle finger to his wrist.

What the bloody hell kind of reaction is that? I wondered, but before I could ask, a bustling from the office drew my attention back. Aria's head popped out.

"Everyone's okay, but it looks like they were all unconscious. They're just waking up now, so we aren't sure what happened to them yet." Her eyes went wide when she saw our father sitting up, and her jaw about hit the floor when he gave her a mock salute. Her head disappeared back inside the room, and I could hear urgent mumbling, though I couldn't make out the words.

A second later, she and Lia stepped out cautiously, and their support crew, clearly dazed, stumbled after.

Tension thrummed through Rhys's hands as he helped me to my feet and pulled me back from the man sitting on the ground grinning at everyone.

I tried to look at his chakras to get a bead on what was happening, but the colors were dim and hazy. It was the same when I looked at my sisters, so I suspected I'd nearly burned my battery out. I squinted, as if that would help me see the ethereal colors more clearly.

"What's going on here?" Treigh demanded, breaking the awkward silence.

"We're all wondering the same thing," Rhys agreed.

"Well, isn't anyone going to help me up?" Dad demanded, daring any one of us to wipe that smirk off his face.

"I hardly think so." I growled.

"How rude." He rolled over onto his hands and knees and slowly pushed himself upright. It was a bit like watching a newborn foal, all knees and elbows.

Maddie stepped forward to put herself between us and the man she'd known so long ago. "Dorian, don't you dare ..."

He cut her off with laughter, and in a way, I understood that. What did poor normie Maddie Alvarez think she could do against him? She bubbled with rage at his condescension, but it only made him laugh harder.

"You should see your face!" he wheezed, nearly doubling over in his mirth. I'd never seen him laugh like this in my life.

"He's gone round the twist," I mumbled, certain that the whirlwind of energy had sucked the sanity right out of him.

That brought on a whole new series of guffaws, until he was gasping for breath. He held up his hand in a *stop* gesture while he tried to slow the air in and out of his lungs. At long last, he drew himself up to his full height, tears of laughter streaming down his cheeks. I strained to see his chakras again, pulling whatever energy I could find up out of my toenails.

Though my Sight was still weak, I could see his crown chakra flashing like a Christmas light.

Coughing back a few residual chuckles, a genuine joy radiated from the man in front of us, and I could see his aura begin to expand, making room for divine energy. I gripped Rhys's hand in terror, knowing none of us had the power left in us to engage in another boss battle.

The divine aura around him began to take shape, but it wasn't Set's shadow I saw. Nor was it Mercury's. It looked like a giant dog. My knees buckled, and I would've gone down if Rhys hadn't been holding me up.

"*David?*" I gasped.

"I have one question," he grinned. "Just how rich am I?"

Chapter 26

David wouldn't tell us anything until he was happily situated in a pizza place awaiting the delivery of several pies. Once the orders were placed and the waitress had retreated to the kitchen, he wrung my father's hands together in a mwah-ha-ha gesture.

"Alright, enough with the suspense," I insisted. "What the bloody hell is going on in there?"

"Okay, okay," he chuffed in Dad's voice and accent. "I'll tell you what I can. While Mercury and Set were duking it out in here," he tapped his temple, "I saw an opening, and I took it."

"What do you mean, you saw an opening?" Rhys was leaning forward, staring intently at David's expression on Dad's face.

"Well, the best way I can explain it is that it looked like some weird holographic video game with ol' Dorian in the middle. They were fighting around him, but he was taking shots, too. There was physical- him and spirit-him, like layered on top of each other. Spirit-him looked right at me and held his hand out. And then this big *space* opened in his middle, and I took his hand, and then I was *in*."

"So you're possessing him, then?" Lia piped up. Treigh and Maddie were sitting so close to her that I was amazed she could even move her arms. She didn't seem to mind, though. "He invited you in?"

"Yeah, I guess."

Aria nodded as if this made sense. "He chose Atonement. He gave David his body to atone for being responsible for David's death."

"Is he ..." I couldn't bring myself to say the word.

"... dead?" David finished for me. "No, he's still in here, but he's sort of sleeping. Dormant. Whatever. I don't know if he'll stay that way, but that's how he is now."

"Are you the Devil or the Magician?" Logan asked.

David whipped the Devil Card out of his shirt pocket. "Just like old times," he laughed. "I didn't find the Magician Card anywhere."

"Must've moved on to someone else," Maddie mused. "But who, I wonder?"

David shrugged. "I don't really care." He turned to me and his eyes turned solemn. "Thanks for telling me to stick with you," he said seriously. "I wouldn't have gotten a second chance otherwise. I'd probably be haunting that construction site."

My throat tightened and I nodded, afraid to speak for fear of being overcome with emotion again.

"What was it like?" Lia asked softly, as though she wasn't sure it was her place to ask, though we all wanted to know.

"Being dead?"

She nodded.

"Well, at first I was really confused. I didn't really know who or where I was. I was just *pissed*, and I couldn't really do anything about it. After a while, I could feel how sad Zora was, and the old man was conflicted, but mostly scared. That just made me madder. But when Zora told me to stay with her, it was like I sort of remembered who I was a little bit, so I did what she said. Then little by little, I started to remember, but I couldn't do anything and no one could see me until you did." He nodded in Lia's direction. "Then I just sort of hung around waiting to see what would happen, and here we are."

"What will you do now?" Logan asked, sipping a sweet tea. He was asking David, but I was thinking about what my answer would be to that same question.

"I don't really know," David answered honestly. "I've never had enough money to do whatever I want, and I'm not always good at playing it smart. I'm thinking I'll stay here in the house for at least a while, until I get everything figured out."

"Won't that be weird, living in a possessed body in the house where you died?" Lia leaned her head against Treigh's shoulder, weariness weighing her down. I could relate.

"I don't know; probably not. Maybe. But ghosts do that all the time, right?"

"I think your situation had a little bit of a happier ending than most," Paul offered, and Logan and Aria nodded in agreement.

"Besides, I actually like it here. I'm hoping Zora will help me learn to adult a little bit so I don't screw up this sweet deal."

"Yeah, I will do. You're basically taking over Dad's identity, so there are definitely some everyday things you'll need to know like bank accounts, and ..."

"And you'll teach me to drive, right? Once I can drive, I'm going to buy a Porsche."

I rolled my eyes, but couldn't keep from smiling. "There are perks to being an adult, but some responsibilities, too. I'll give you the crash course."

"It's a trade-off," he acknowledged.

"I could help, if you need me to," Maddie offered. "I've done a lot more adulting than any of you."

"I bet Aunt Pam would help, too." Aria was the most relaxed I'd ever seen her, which sort of made sense, given the circumstances of pretty much every single interaction we'd had to date.

"I just had a weird thought," Lia mused. "In a way, the ritual did work, just not the way Blair intended for it to." She looked around the table. "Five of the Arcana have been united. The difference is that none of us are bound."

"I'm still in favor of world domination," David joked.

"Too soon," Aria chuckled.

"Don't knock it till you've tried it," he persisted. I had to admit that I had missed the kid. It felt good to have his sarcasm back.

"Lord, yes," Treigh exclaimed, and I was confused until I spotted the procession of servers approaching with our pizzas. "I need some food therapy right about now."

There was a murmur of vehement agreement as the steaming pies were set on the table and the scent of tomatoes and garlic hung thick over the table. Talking took a back seat to stuffing our faces for the next several minutes, and I was pretty sure a gooey, cheesy pepperoni-laden slice had never tasted so good.

***

We agreed to meet up the next day, but all of us were completely knackered and needed sleep, so once dinner was over we all went our separate ways. I drove Dad's car since David had no idea how to, though he was more than willing to give it a go. I swung by the church parking lot where Rhys's rolling home waited.

"Why don't you pull Priscilla into the driveway, and you can stay at the house tonight?" I offered to Rhys.

"Sounds great. Luxury isn't really my style, but I think I've earned a day or two of convalescence."

"Stay as long as you want," David added. "We've got lots of cool video games and streaming movies, and ..."

"Whoa, slow your roll there, partner," our older brother laughed. "Right now, all I can think about is a shower and a bed. Electronics will have to wait."

"How long will you stay?" Rhys had really been my first—and my only—friend, and I wasn't eager to see him go.

"Oh, I don't know. Maybe a few days. I don't tend to stay anywhere too long, you know." I think he could sense my disappointment. "But I'm only a text away, you know. You could even travel with me someday, if you want." He included both of us in the invitation, but I felt like the comment was really meant for me.

"That'd be *awesome*," David gushed as we pulled into the drive.

"Do you think, maybe," I began hesitantly, "you might come back with your mom at Christmas? I haven't had a proper Christmas in a long time." The only perfect memory from my childhood still pulled at me, and I clung to it, hoping to re-create some of that feeling of wholeness.

Rhys studied me for a moment before getting out of the SUV. "Christmas sounds good. Maybe our sisters can come, too."

For the first time in almost forever, I felt a *ping* in my heart chakra which tasted like hope and joy and freedom.

I truly hope that you've enjoyed the Arcana Trilogy. If you've joined me on this journey for hundreds and hundreds of pages, thank you. Your support, my readers, means everything!
If you feel I've served you well as your storyteller, please consider posting spoiler-free reviews for these books on Amazon, Goodreads,

or anywhere that will help other readers become acquainted with these wonderful characters.

With eternal gratitude, JB Caine

www.ingramcontent.com/pod-product-compliance
Lightning Source LLC
Chambersburg PA
CBHW060326260626
47160CB00007B/2697